Heartland™

Taking Chances

Lauren Brooke

SCHOLASTIC

With special thanks to Linda Chapman

To my parents, for buying me my first pony
and making my dreams come true.

Scholastic Children's Books,
Commonwealth House, 1-19 New Oxford Street,
London WC1A 1NU, UK
a division of Scholastic Ltd
London ~ New York ~ Toronto ~ Sydney ~ Auckland
Mexico City ~ New Delhi ~ Hong Kong

Published in the UK by Scholastic Ltd, 2001
Series created by Working Partners Ltd

ISBN 0 439 99848 4

Typeset by TW Typesetting, Midsomer Norton, Somerset
Printed and bound by Nørhaven Paperback A/S, Denmark

8 10 9

Chapter One

Amy finished filling up a water bucket and glanced at her watch. It was twelve-thirty. Soraya would be arriving any minute. She deposited the bucket in Solo's stall and went up to the top of the drive to wait for her friend.

On either side of the driveway, horses and ponies grazed contentedly in the turn-out paddocks, the October breeze ruffling their coats and sending the occasional red or gold leaf skittering across the short grass.

Only one paddock was empty. In the middle of it stood a single oak sapling, the soil still fresh around its base.

Amy walked over to the wooden gate. "Pegasus," she whispered, a wave of sadness flooding over her as she looked at the young tree. She could hardly believe it was really only three weeks since Pegasus had been buried there.

"Oh, Pegasus." Amy pictured the great grey horse.

In his younger days, he had been one of the most famous show-jumpers in the world. But Amy remembered him better as the horse who had let her play round his legs when she was little, and who had nuzzled her when she was upset. To her, he was the horse whose strong presence had helped her through the nightmare of her mom being killed in a road accident four months ago, and the horse who had been her friend.

Amy swallowed as she looked at the sapling. *Everything's changed so much in the last few months*, she thought to herself. *Mom's gone. Pegasus's gone. Lou's come back.*

Lou's return to Heartland was one of the few good things to have happened. Until recently, Amy's older sister had worked in Manhattan, but since their mom's death she had decided to leave her banking job and live permanently at Heartland – the equine sanctuary their mom, Marion, had set up on their grandpa's farm.

The sound of a car coming up the drive roused Amy from her thoughts. She looked round.

Soraya Martin, her best friend, was waving madly from the front passenger seat as her mom's car came up the drive. Amy took a deep breath, swallowing hard and pushing down the ache of painful memories. She waved back – forcing herself to smile, burying her inner sadness.

"Hi!" Soraya called, winding down the window. "Sorry I'm late. Mom had to pick up some groceries on the way over." The car drew to a halt and Soraya jumped out, black curls bouncing on her shoulders. "See you later, Mom," she said. "Thanks for the ride."

"Sure," Mrs Martin said, smiling at Amy. "Now, you girls have fun."

Amy and Soraya grinned at each other. "We will," they both said at once.

Half an hour later, Amy tightened her fingers on Sundance's reins and looked towards the fallen tree that lay across one side of the trail. "Come on then, boy," she whispered. "Let's jump it!"

"Be careful, Amy," Soraya called. "It's a big one."

"Not for Sundance," Amy replied, turning her buckskin pony towards the tree trunk.

Seeing the jump, Sundance threw his head up in excitement and plunged forward, but Amy was ready for him. Her body moved effortlessly in the saddle. "Easy now," she murmured, her fingers caressing his warm neck.

The pony's golden ears flickered as he listened to her voice – and then he relaxed, his neck lowering and his mouth softening on the bit.

Amy squeezed with her legs. In five strides they reached the tree trunk. It loomed up in front of them, massive and solid. Amy felt Sundance's muscles bunch as he met the take-off stride perfectly and rose gracefully into the air. Amy caught a glimpse of thick, gnarled bark flashing by beneath them, felt a moment of suspension as if she and Sundance were flying, and then heard the sweet thud of his hooves as he landed cleanly on the other side. They were over!

"Good boy!" Amy cried in delight.

"That was so cool!" Soraya said, letting Jasmine trot forward to meet them. "He's jumping better than ever, Amy."

"I know!" Amy grinned, patting Sundance's neck. "He's incredible!"

As the two ponies reached each other, Jasmine stretched out her neck to say hello. With an angry squeal, Sundance threw his head in the air, his ears back. "Stop it, Sundance!" Amy exclaimed, turning him away. "Jasmine's your friend."

The buckskin nuzzled her leg affectionately. He was bad-tempered with most horses and people, but adored Amy. She had first seen him at a horse-sale. Thin and unhappy, he attacked anyone who tried to come through the gate of his pen, until Amy had persuaded her mom to buy him. They took him back to Heartland, where Amy gradually gained his trust and affection.

"Have you got any shows planned for him?" Soraya asked, as they started along the trail again.

Amy shook her head. "There's just no time. All the stalls have been full since the open day and there's a waiting list of people who want to bring their horses to us."

Just two weeks ago, Lou had organized an open day at Heartland. People had been invited to come along and find out about the methods that Heartland used to cure physically and emotionally damaged horses. Amy, and Ty – Heartland's seventeen-year-old stable-hand – had given demonstrations, and the day had been a great success. Ever since then, they had been inundated with enquiries from owners with problem horses.

"It's good that you've got lots of horses boarding, though," Soraya said. "I mean, it must be such a relief to know that you can carry on your mom's work and not stress too much about money."

Amy nodded, mulling over the difficulties Heartland had faced before the open day. After her mom had died, Heartland had come close to shutting down because of the lack of customers and funding, but now, thankfully, it was different. Business was booming.

"Yeah, I'm glad we're busy," she said. "Even if it does mean that I don't have much time to compete." She patted Sundance's neck. "Still, I guess things may start getting easier now Ben will be working for us."

Ben was the nephew of Lisa Stillman, the wealthy and successful owner of Fairfield Arabian Stud. After Amy had cured one of Fairfield's show horses, Lisa had been so impressed that she had arranged for Ben to come and work at Heartland in order for him to learn their methods. He was due to arrive that afternoon.

Soraya glanced at Amy. "Do you reckon he's got a girlfriend?"

"Why?" Amy grinned. "Are you interested?" She and Soraya had both met Ben when he had dropped off the problem horse that Amy had treated. Tall and good-looking, he had seemed OK – although not really Amy's type.

"You have to admit he *is* cute," Soraya said. She raised her eyebrows. "Poor guy. I guess he's not going to know anyone round here. Maybe I'll just *have* to offer to show him around."

Amy feigned innocence. "Don't put yourself out, Soraya. I'm sure Ty can do it – he's looking forward to having another guy around the place."

"Oh *no*," Soraya said quickly. "I'm sure I'd make a *much* better guide than Ty."

"Well, I'm looking forward to seeing Ben's horse," Amy said. "He's a show-jumper. Ben said he'd only work at Heartland if his horse could come too."

"So what time's he arriving?" Soraya asked.

"Two o'clock."

Soraya glanced at her watch. "We should get a move on then. It's almost one-thirty."

Amy gathered up her reins. "What are you waiting for? Let's go!"

Amy and Soraya rode down the trail that led to the back of Heartland. Coming out of the trees, they could see Heartland's barns and sheds spread out before them – the turn-out paddocks with their dark wooden fencing, the two training rings, the twelve-stall back barn, and the front stable block that made an L-shape with the white, weather-boarded farmhouse.

As Amy halted Sundance she heard the sound of hooves thudding angrily against the wall of the barn.

"Steady now!" Ty's raised voice could be heard from inside the barn. "Easy, girl!"

"It sounds like Ty could use some help," she said.

"You go," Soraya said. "I'll see to Sundance."

"Thanks." Amy threw Sundance's reins at her friend and headed into the barn. A wide aisle separated the six stalls on each side. From a stall near the back came the crash of hooves striking the wall. Amy realized it was Dancer's stall.

Dancer was a paint mare who had been half starved and left on a tiny patch of land. When the animal charity that had found her called them, Amy and Ty had immediately agreed to help. The mare had arrived two days ago and her treatment was progressing slowly.

"You OK, Ty?" Amy called.

Ty looked over Dancer's half-door. His dark hair was dishevelled. "Just about," he replied, wiping his bare forearm across his face.

"What's up?" Amy asked, looking into the stall. Dancer was standing by the back wall, her body trembling.

"All I did was pick up her hoof and she just went crazy," Ty said, shaking his head. "She broke her lead-rope and started acting like she was trying to kick the stall down. She had me cornered for a few moments, but luckily she didn't get me. Now she's in a total state."

Amy looked at the frightened mare. "How about using

some chestnut powder to calm her down," she suggested, remembering it had been one of her mom's favourite remedies for upset horses.

Ty nodded. "Good idea. You wait with her while I fetch it," he said, and then hurried off.

The mare shifted uneasily at the back of the stall. Her muscles were tense and her ribs stuck painfully through her staring coat. Around her face were scars where a halter had been digging into the skin, and around her fetlocks were rope-burns from the too-tight hobbles that had been tied around her legs to stop her from wandering away.

"It's OK, girl," Amy said softly. "You're safe now that you're here. No one's going to hurt you any more."

The mare's ears flickered uncertainly.

Ty returned with a small tin. He handed it to Amy. "Here," he said. "It might be best if you try. Perhaps I remind her of her last owner."

Amy unscrewed the lid of the tin. Inside, there was a gritty grey powder. Taking a little, she rubbed it on to the palms of her hands. Then she stepped forward, her shoulders turned sideways to the mare, her eyes lowered.

Dancer moved nervously. Amy stopped, offered her palm for the mare to sniff, and waited.

After a few moments, the mare turned and snorted. Stretching her muzzle out towards Amy's upturned hand, she breathed in, her nostrils dilating. Amy waited a few moments, and then, talking softly, she gently reached out and touched

Dancer's neck with her other hand. As her fingers stroked and caressed, she felt the mare gradually begin to relax. Amy's fingers worked the mare's neck until she came to her head. When Dancer did not object, she took hold of the lead-rope.

"Good work," Ty said in a low voice. Rubbing a little of the powder on to his own palms, he approached the mare. She looked at him cautiously, but then stretched out her head and let him stroke her too. "Poor girl," he said, rubbing her neck. "Your life hasn't been too great up to now, has it?"

"Well, it's going to be a lot better from here on in," Amy said.

For a moment they stood in silence, both stroking the mare.

Amy looked at the deep scars on Dancer's brown and white legs. "Maybe when you touched her feet she thought that you were going to hobble her," she suggested.

Ty nodded. "I guess we'll just have to take things slowly with her."

"As always," Amy said, smiling at him.

She didn't know what she'd do without Ty. He was so good with the horses, and after her mom had died he had taken over the running of the yard while the family came to terms with their loss. She knew they were lucky to have him. He never seemed to treat working at Heartland as just a regular job – for Ty it was a way of life.

Ty looked at the tin in his hand. "Your mom's magic powder comes up trumps again."

Amy nodded. Her mom had been told about the powder by an old horseman in Tennessee. It contained herbs ground up with chestnut trimmings – the horny growths that grew on the inside of horse's legs and were snipped off by the farrier when they grew too long. Marion, her mom, had noted down the recipe and they had used it at Heartland ever since.

"Your mom was amazing," Ty said, turning the tin over in his hands. "She knew so much. Sometimes I wonder if I'll ever be as good as her, if I'll ever have half as much knowledge as she did."

"You're pretty good already, Ty," Amy said in surprise.

"But not good enough," Ty said. He shook his head. "I was learning so much from her, Amy. Sometimes I feel that what I know is just the tip of an enormous iceberg. And I hate it. I can't stop thinking that if only I knew more I might be capable of helping horses more effectively."

"But you mustn't think like that, Ty," Amy said quickly. She stepped closer, wanting to let him know that she understood. "I felt the same when Pegasus was really ill and I couldn't help him. But then I realized I just had to accept that there are things I don't know and that all I can do is try my best." She paused, her eyes searching his. "You know Mom would have said the same."

Ty nodded slowly. "Yeah, I guess."

They stood for a moment, neither of them speaking.

The silence was interrupted by the sound of footsteps

running down the aisle. "Hey, you guys! There's a trailer coming up the drive!" Soraya reached Dancer's door and looked over. "It's really fancy and smart. Come and check it out."

"It must be Ben," Amy said, looking at Ty.

He nodded. Leaving Dancer, they hurried down the yard. A gleaming white trailer, with green and purple stripes and a purple crest, and the words "Fairfield Arabian Stud" emblazoned on the jockey door, was pulling up in front of the house. The truck stopped and Ben Stillman jumped out.

"Hi there," he said, straightening his tall frame.

Amy stepped forward. "Hi, I'm Amy Fleming. We met when you brought Promise over here for your aunt. This is my friend, Soraya Martin," she said, pushing Soraya forward.

"Hi," Soraya grinned.

"Yeah, I remember," Ben smiled. "Hi."

"And you've met Ty," Amy said.

"Welcome to Heartland." Ty offered his hand.

As they shook hands, the farmhouse door opened and Lou came out. She too had met Ben when he'd dropped Promise off at Heartland. "Hello again," she said, smiling at Ben.

"Good to meet you properly this time," Ben said.

"I'll see you later – I'm just off into town," Lou said, walking off towards her car.

Just then, from inside the trailer came the sound of a horse stamping impatiently.

"Sounds like Red wants to get out," Ben said.

"Here, I'll give you a hand," Ty volunteered.

Ben disappeared inside the trailer while Ty unbolted the ramp. Amy watched eagerly, wondering what Ben's horse would be like.

Ty lowered the ramp to the ground. There was a clatter of hooves and suddenly a bright chestnut horse shot nervously down the ramp, with Ben holding tightly on to the end of its lead-rope. Once out, the horse stopped dead and looked around, his head held high.

"Wow!" Amy exclaimed. "He's gorgeous!"

"He's called Red," Ben said, looking pleased. "He's a Thoroughbred-Hanoverian cross."

Amy walked closer, admiring Red's handsome head, close-coupled back and strong, clean legs. Standing, she guessed, at around sixteen-two hands, he looked every inch a show-jumper. "How old is he?" she asked, letting Red sniff her hand and then patting his muscular neck.

"Six," Ben said. "My aunt brought him for me when he was three." He glanced at the trailer. "I guess there are *some* advantages to having a rich aunt who's into horses."

Hearing a strange note in his voice, Amy glanced at him. For a moment she saw a look of bitterness cross his face.

"*Some* advantages?" Ty said. He was putting the ramp up and obviously hadn't seen Ben's expression. "That's the understatement of the year!"

"Yeah." Ben coughed, his face suddenly clearing and his

voice becoming light again. "I guess you're right. So, which stall should I put him in?" he asked Amy.

"The one at the end," Amy replied, pointing towards the stable block. "It's all bedded down ready for him."

Ben clicked his tongue and Red moved forward.

Leaving Soraya and Ty to sort out the trailer, Amy went on ahead of Ben and opened the stall door. "Do you compete much on Red?" she asked.

Ben nodded as he set about taking off the wraps that had protected the gelding's legs on the journey over. "He's got real talent. I've been taking him in Prelim Jumper classes, but with the way he's been winning I figure he's going to upgrade real quick." He stood up with the wraps in his arms. "We're going to make it to the top," he said confidently. "I'm sure of it."

Amy looked at him in surprise; he didn't sound like he had any doubts.

"So," Ben said, walking out of the stall. "What's it like living in this area?"

"OK," Amy replied.

"You'll have to show me around," Ben said.

Amy remembered what Soraya had said and saw the perfect opportunity. "Well, I'm always pretty busy with the horses," she said, as they walked down the yard towards where Soraya and Ty were standing by the trailer. "But Soraya has loads of spare time."

"Did I hear my name?" Soraya said, turning to face them.

"Yeah, I was just telling Ben that you'd be happy to show him around," Amy answered, giving her a meaningful look.

"Yeah, of course!" Soraya said, stepping forward eagerly. "Any time."

"Thanks." Ben smiled at her. "I might just take you up on that."

"Do you want to see round the yard?" Amy offered. "You've got all the horses to meet and then we can start telling you about our work here at Heartland."

"Actually, you know, I might leave all that sort of stuff till tomorrow," Ben said, yawning. "I could do with going back to my lodgings and unpacking. Then I think I'll just crash for a while."

"Oh ... right," Amy said, a bit taken aback. She knew that if she was about to start work at a new yard then the first thing she would want to do was to look at the horses. "Well, sure. Go ahead."

"Great," Ben said. "Well, I'll just unload Red's kit, then I'll be off."

Amy, Ty and Soraya helped him carry the mountain of rugs, tack and grooming kit up to the tack-room and then Ben unhitched the trailer and got into the truck. "I'll be back to feed Red later," he said, starting the engine.

Not long after he had driven off, Lou got back. "I think I just passed Ben on the road. Has he gone already?" she asked, getting out of her car.

Amy nodded.

"But I was going to ask him if he wanted to stay for supper tonight," Lou said, frowning. "Oh well, I guess I can give him a call. I've got his phone number." She looked at Soraya and Ty. "You're both welcome to stay too."

"That would be great," Ty said. "Thanks."

"Unfortunately, I can't," Soraya said ruefully. "I'm going out tonight for my mom's birthday. But thanks anyway, Lou."

Lou looked down the drive. "It's a bit odd that Ben didn't stick around for longer. I thought he'd be here for hours. Grandpa will be sorry to have missed him." Shaking her head, she went back into the house.

"So what do you think of him?" Amy asked Ty and Soraya, as they walked back up the yard.

"Definitely cute!" Soraya enthused.

"And after all, what else matters?" Ty teased.

Soraya pretended to punch him.

Amy grinned. "Come on, what do you think, Ty?"

"He seems fine," Ty said, shrugging.

"Yes ... and?" Amy pushed for more

"And nothing," Ty said. He looked at Amy and Soraya's expectant faces. "Well, what else do you expect me to say?" he demanded. "I've only met the guy for about five minutes."

"Well, I've only met him for five minutes too, and I think he seems really nice," Amy said. She turned to Soraya. "He was telling me about Red. He's been competing in Prelim Jumpers. Ben thinks they'll upgrade pretty quick."

"I wonder when we'll get to see him ride," Soraya said. Her eyes looked dreamy. "He's so fit and athletic!"

Ty grimaced. "Oh, please!" Rolling his eyes at them, he went into the tack-room.

Exchanging grins, Amy and Soraya followed him. In the middle of the tack-room floor was a mound of Ben's stuff.

"Three saddles," Ty commented, starting to make space on the already crowded saddle racks.

"And all top quality," Amy added, picking up a forward-cut jumping saddle and admiring the supple, well-oiled leather.

"I wish I had a rich aunt who would buy me a horse like Red, and all this stuff," Soraya said

Ty nodded as he hung up a bridle. "Ben sure is a lucky guy."

Amy thought about the look she had seen pass across Ben's face just after he'd unloaded Red. At that moment he hadn't seemed exactly thrilled with his good fortune. Still, it must have been wonderful to have grown up on a huge stud farm with lots of money. Perhaps he'd just found it difficult leaving Fairfield and was feeling upset with his aunt. "Imagine living at a place like Fairfield," she said out loud.

"Yeah," Ty said nodding. "I wish."

Amy looked at him. Ty's family had very little money. To help out his parents he had first started working as a part-time stable-hand at Heartland when he was just fifteen. Then he had left school a year later, when he was offered a full-time position by Marion Fleming.

"Do you know why Ben grew up with his aunt instead of his parents?" Soraya asked.

"I think it was something to do with his parents getting divorced when he was younger," Amy said, remembering a conversation between Lou and Lisa Stillman when they'd first discussed the possibility of Ben coming to Heartland. "But I don't really know that much about it. Still, I guess we might find out more tonight."

"I wish I could stay," Soraya said longingly. "Promise you'll find out all the gossip about him – like whether he's got a girlfriend or not."

"Oh, you mean the really *important* stuff!" Amy grinned at her. "Don't worry, of course I will."

Chapter Two

Ben arrived back at Heartland just as Amy and Ty were mixing up the evening feeds. "Did you get unpacked?" Ty asked, when he joined them in the feed-room.

Ben nodded. "Yeah, thanks." He looked round at the huge metal bins, stone-flagged floor and wooden ceiling-beams. "So this is where you keep the grain, right?"

"Yeah," Amy said. "Just help yourself to whatever you want for Red. There's cod-liver oil and other supplements in the cupboard over there." She pointed to a corner of the feed-room, "And you can use any of those buckets in that pile – they're all spare."

"Here," Ty said, getting a bucket for him.

"Thanks," Ben said, "but I've brought Red his own buckets. They're in the trailer."

He returned a few minutes later with a couple of steel buckets, each embossed with the Fairfield crest and with

Red's name in neat black lettering on the side. Ben scooped some oats and alfalfa cubes into one of the buckets and then looked in the cupboard.

"Wow!" he exclaimed, staring at the packed shelves, laden with dried herbs and country remedies – honey, bicarbonate of soda, vinegar, chalk. "You sure use a lot of supplements here."

"Well, we don't just use herbs as feed supplements," Amy said. "We use them to help deal with behavioural and physical problems. If you like, when we've finished feeding Ty and I can start giving you an idea of what some of the herbs do, can't we, Ty?"

"Sure," Ty said enthusiastically. "You'll be amazed at the healing properties some of them have."

"Yeah, maybe some other time," Ben said casually. "I think I'll go see Red now." Quickly mixing up a feed, he carried it out of the feed-room.

Amy frowned at Ty. "That's strange. I'd have thought he would have been really interested. After all, he is here to learn about what we do." From the yard, she could hear the horses in the front stable block banging their doors impatiently. They would have seen Ben walk past with Red's bucket. "And he could have offered to help us feed the other horses," she said, feeling slightly irritated. "Now the others are going to go wild until they get fed."

"I know what you mean," Ty shrugged. "But he's only just arrived and probably wants to make sure Red's settling in."

"I guess," Amy said. She picked up a pile of buckets. "Well, we'd better get feeding before those stalls are all kicked down."

At seven o'clock, Lou came out on the yard. "Dinner's almost ready!" she called.

Amy and Ty came out of the tack-room just as Ben appeared from Red's stall.

"How is he?" Ty asked.

"Settling in just fine," Ben replied, walking down the yard with them.

A delicious smell of baked ham filled the kitchen. Jack Bartlett, Amy and Lou's grandfather, was draining a pan of black-eyed peas at the sink. "Hi," he said to Ben, turning and offering his hand. "Jack Bartlett."

"Pleased to meet you, sir," Ben said, shaking hands.

As Ty and Amy began to set the table and Lou fixed them all drinks, Ben spent a few moments looking at the photographs that covered the kitchen walls.

"Is this your mom in these pictures?" he asked Amy.

She nodded and joined him by the pine dresser. "Yeah, that was her competing in England. We lived there when I was small."

"So why did you move back here?" Ben said.

"Because of Daddy's accident," Amy said.

"Oh, my aunt told me about that," Ben said. "He was riding in a jump-off, wasn't he?"

Amy nodded. Her father had been riding Pegasus in the World Championships. Pegasus had caught his legs in the top bar and fallen. Both he and her father had been badly injured. Having been only three at the time, Amy had no real memory of the event. But as Ben spoke, she saw Lou look round and frown. Lou had been eleven and Amy knew she remembered it all much more clearly.

"So what happened to your dad after the accident?" Ben asked Amy.

"He damaged his spine and was in a wheelchair for a bit," Amy explained. "Although he did get better, the doctors said that it would be too dangerous for him to ever ride again." Her voice hardened. "He couldn't cope with the situation and so he ran off – abandoning us and leaving the horses. He obviously didn't want anything to do with us any more, and so Mom decided to move back here to live with Grandpa."

"That's not exactly true, Amy!"

Amy turned. Lou was staring angrily at her. "Dad did try to get back together with Mom. And you know it – we found that letter, remember!"

How could Amy forget? It had been a real shock when she and Lou had been clearing out Marion's room and found a letter from their dad, begging their mom for a reconciliation.

Lou's blue eyes flashed. "If Mom had stayed in England instead of 'running off' as you put it, then maybe there'd have been a chance that they *would* have got back together!"

"You don't know that," Amy said hotly. "And what was

Mom supposed to do? Hang around waiting until Daddy decided he was good and ready?"

"Yes! That's precisely what she should have done!" Lou exclaimed.

"Amy! Lou!" Jack Bartlett said, stepping forward. "That's enough!" His voice softened. "I know both of you have strong feelings, but a lot of stuff went on at the time that neither of you know about – don't judge your parents now."

Lou turned abruptly and went back to the sideboard. Amy knew that her sister didn't feel the same about their father as she did. Devastated by his disappearance, Lou had refused to accept that he wasn't coming back. When Marion had told them of her plans to move back to Virginia, she had refused to go, begging to be allowed to stay on at her English boarding school instead. When their mom had been alive, Lou had made it abundantly clear that she saw the move to Virginia as a betrayal of their father.

Ben cleared his throat. "So your mom came here to live?" he said, breaking the silence.

Amy spoke more quietly. "Yeah, Mom came here with Pegasus. He was emotionally traumatized, and conventional medicine was only helping his physical wounds, so she began to explore alternative therapies. Pegasus recovered, and then Mom started Heartland to put into practice the methods she had learnt – with the aim of helping other horses."

"I see," Ben said. "And your mom never competed again?" he asked.

"No, she was far more interested in her work here."

"How about you?" Ben asked, sitting down. "Do you compete, Amy?"

"Occasionally," Amy replied. "When I get the time, I take Sundance, my pony, in the Large Pony Hunter division."

"And what about you, Ty?" Ben asked.

"No," Ty said. "I'm not interested."

"Not at all?" Ben said, looking surprised.

Ty shook his head. "I've had a few people offer me rides on horses but competing doesn't really do it for me. I find working with damaged horses far more satisfying."

Amy smiled at Ty, knowing just how he felt.

Ben didn't look as if he understood this at all. "I just couldn't be like that," he said, shaking his head. "I mean, how do you prove that you're really good at what you do? At least in the ring everyone gets to see your talent with horses."

Ty shrugged. "I guess I just don't care that much about what other people think."

For a moment, Ty and Ben's eyes met and Amy felt a certain tension creep into the air.

"OK, folks," Jack Bartlett announced. "Dinner's ready."

With the sudden bustle of movement, the tension dissolved. Chair-legs scraped as they all sat down, and Lou began to hand out platefuls of baked ham, a basket of cornbread and a bowl heaped with black-eyed peas.

"This looks incredible," Ben said, helping himself.

"I'd like to propose a toast to the latest addition to Heartland," Jack Bartlett said, lifting his glass when everyone's plate was piled high. "Welcome, Ben," he said. "And I hope you'll have a very happy time here."

Everyone raised their glasses. "To Ben!" they all echoed.

Ben raised his glass back with an easy smile. "To Heartland," he said.

When Amy's alarm clock rang as usual at six o'clock the next morning, she hit the off-button with a groan. She hadn't got to bed until after midnight and the last thing she felt like doing right now was leaping up to face the day. However, as always, the horses were waiting.

Yawning, she climbed out of bed, and with eyes half closed pulled on her jeans. Not bothering to brush her long hair, she went downstairs and slipped on her boots.

Going out on to the yard, she thought about Ben. He had been a fun guest to have over for dinner. He had talked to Lou about her old job in Manhattan and to Grandpa about his farming days. Amy had even managed to find out from him that he wasn't dating anyone – a piece of information that she knew would please Soraya tremendously.

She had refilled the water buckets and just started to mix the feeds when Ty arrived. "Morning," he said, coming into the feed-room. "Any sign of Ben yet?"

Amy shook her head as she added scoopfuls of soaked beet to the grain in the buckets. "No." Ben was supposed to start work at seven o'clock, the same as Ty, but he hadn't arrived. "He'll probably be here any minute," she said.

However, Ben's truck didn't appear until almost eight-thirty. Hearing the engine, Amy looked out of the stall she was mucking out.

"Hi, there!" Ben said, jumping out of the truck. "Great morning, isn't it?" he said enthusiastically.

Amy had expected him to be full of apologies for being so late. "Yeah, I guess so," she replied.

Ben seemed to sense her reserve. "Hey, sorry I'm a little late," he said. "You don't really mind, do you? I overslept a bit."

"It's OK," Amy said, pushing down the little voice in her head that was suggesting that maybe that an hour and a half was more than a *little* late.

"OK, then," Ben said. "What do you want me to do?"

"I guess I should show you where things are first," Amy said. "And then you can help Ty and me. After we've finished mucking out the stalls, we sweep the yard and then groom and exercise until lunchtime. Come on, I'll introduce you to the horses."

"Hang on a sec," Ben said. "I'll just say hi to Red."

Amy waited patiently as Ben went up to the tall chestnut and patted him, speaking to him in a quiet voice. Amy watched the horse nuzzle Ben's shoulder. He obviously adored his owner.

Ben joined her after a few minutes and she began to take

him round the stalls. "This is Jake," she said, stroking the bay Clydesdale in the stall next to Red's. "He's twenty-one." Jake pushed hopefully against her hand; taking the hint, she fished out a packet of mints from her pocket. "Mom rescued him at a horse sale," Amy explained. "He's got bad arthritis and can't be re-homed."

"How many horses do you have here?" Ben asked.

"There are seven liveries and ten rescue horses," Amy said. "Eight of the rescues will hopefully recover enough to be found new homes. Two of them are here permanently – Jake and my pony, Sundance." She kissed Jake's nose. "I hate saying goodbye to horses when they leave. You get so attached to them." She glanced at Ben to see if he understood, but he was already moving on to the next stall.

"That's Gypsy Queen," she said, going after him. "She's here to be cured of her habit of bucking." She was about to explain more about Gypsy's history, but Ben was walking on again.

He showed a similar lack of interest when Amy began explaining to him about the different therapies they used at Heartland. She showed him the medicine cabinet filled with her mom's books, herbal treatments, aromatherapy oils and Bach Flower Remedies.

"What's the point of all this?" Ben said at last. "I mean, why not just trust the vet?"

"We do," Amy said. "It's just that Mom believed that you can use natural remedies to complement traditional medicine and our vet, Scott, is of pretty much the same opinion." She saw the sceptical look on Ben's face. "Our methods *do* work, you know. Don't forget, we cured Promise when nobody else managed it."

"I suppose," Ben said, but he still looked less than convinced. He stepped towards the door. "You said the stalls needed finishing off. Shall I get started? Ty looked like he could use some help."

Amy nodded and Ben strode off.

Amy stared after him, feeling confused. Lisa was paying for Ben to be at Heartland but he didn't seem at all interested in their work – in fact, he didn't even seem to believe that their methods could help.

When they stopped for lunch, Ben fetched his grooming kit and tack. "Aren't you going to have something to eat?" Amy asked.

"I'll ride first," Ben replied, heading in the direction of Red's stall.

"So what do you think of him now?" Amy said to Ty as they went into the kitchen.

"What – apart from him turning up an hour and a half late, taking two hours to muck out four stalls and not taking an interest in the work we do here?" Ty replied dryly.

Amy smiled. "Yeah, despite that. What do you think?"

Ty shrugged. "I don't know. Ask me in a week or so."

As Amy made herself a sandwich, she looked out of the

window and saw Ben walking Red up the track to the school. "Shall we go and watch him ride?" she said.

Ty nodded and, taking their lunch with them, they went up to the training ring.

Ben was cantering Red in a figure of eight. The chestnut was moving lightly and fluently and he executed a perfect flying change in the centre of the ring. Amy saw Ben stroke Red's neck, his lips moving in praise as they cantered on, his body still in the saddle, his back straight, and his hands maintaining a light, steady contact with the horse's mouth.

"He's good," she said in a low voice to Ty.

Seemingly oblivious to their presence, Ben turned Red down the centre of the ring where there was a four-foot jump. With hardly a change in his stride pattern, Red approached and cleared it as easily as if it had been a fence half the height. To Amy, watching at the gate, the bond between horse and rider was unmistakable.

As Ben cantered past, he seemed to notice them for the first time. In one easy transition, he brought Red from a canter to a walk. "Hi, there," he said, circling Red back towards them.

"Hi," Ty replied.

"You jumped that well," Amy said.

Ben smiled. "Thanks." He patted Red. "I thought I might take him out on a trail ride for a bit. Do either of you feel like coming out? I could do with learning about the trails round here."

"Sure, I'll come out on Sundance," Amy said. She glanced at Ty. "How about you? Are you going to come?"

"I'd better not," Ty said. "Solo, Charlie and Moochie need working in the ring and we're not even halfway through the grooming yet."

"You're right." Amy felt guilty. "Maybe I should stay."

"No, it's OK. You go," Ty said. "Ben needs to be shown around and Sundance could use the exercise."

"Great, that's settled then," Ben said, looking at Amy. "I'll walk Red round and cool him off while you get ready."

"Are you sure you don't mind?" Amy asked Ty, as Ben walked Red away.

"It's fine," Ty replied. "You just go ahead and enjoy yourself," he teased. "Don't worry about me. I'll stay and do all the work – as usual."

"That would be right," Amy said with a grin. "I never do a thing round here."

"You said it." Ty said, dodging quickly as she swung a punch at him.

As Amy walked to the ponies' turn-out field to catch Sundance, she felt another flicker of guilt. Now that they had so many horses boarding, Ty was working harder than ever – never taking his days off and often working until late in the evening. *Oh well*, she thought as she reached the paddock gate and called to Sundance, *now Ben's here to help, things will hopefully start getting easier for Ty – for both of us*.

It took her only five minutes to run a brush over

Sundance's coat and tack up. She mounted and went up to the ring. "I'm ready."

"Great," Ben said. "Let's go."

They rode out of the yard on to Teak's Hill, the wooded mountain that rose up behind Heartland. Just before the trail left the fields and entered the trees, Amy stopped Sundance. "I love this view," she said, looking at Heartland stretched out below them, the barns and paddocks bathed in the glow of the October sun.

"It's definitely beautiful up here," Ben said, looking round.

"Your aunt's barn is a great place too," Amy said. "It must have been pretty neat to grow up there."

"Yeah," Ben said, with the hint of a dry, unamused laugh. "I guess it was."

Amy glanced at him.

Ben gathered up his reins. "So, what are we waiting for?" he said, trotting Red on. "I thought you were supposed to be showing me round."

Amy trotted after him. Patches of sunlight filtered through the tree tops and dappled the shady track. "That leads up to Clairdale Ridge," Amy said, pointing out the trail as they rode passed. "And the trail we're going to take, up here on the left, leads down to the creek."

They approached the fallen tree that Sundance had jumped the day before. Seeing it, the buckskin broke into an excited canter.

"I might jump that," Ben said. "Is it safe?"

"Yeah, fine," Amy said, holding Sundance back. She let Ben go first and watched as he cantered Red towards the tree trunk. As he reached it, the young horse spooked at the unfamiliar jump and stopped.

Amy caught her breath as Ben brought his crop down on Red's neck. With a snort, the chestnut shot backwards, head in the air. Clamping his legs on the horse's sides, Ben turned again at the tree trunk. Amy saw the horse's ears prick forward in alarm and his stride shorten as his muscles tensed.

"Go on!" Ben said angrily.

"Ben! He's scared!" Amy exclaimed, as the chestnut began to plunge on the spot.

"He has to learn," Ben shouted back.

Amy cantered over. "Don't upset him. I can give you a lead on Sundance if you want."

Ben ignored her. Using his heels and his seat, he urged Red forward. The horse plunged towards the tree. Amy saw Ben bring his stick down on the horse's shoulder and Red took off in a massive leap. As they landed on the other side, Ben patted Red's shoulder and praised him. "Good boy!" He turned triumphantly to Amy. "See? He had to learn."

But did he have to learn in such a way? Amy thought, looking at the sweat that had broken out on the chestnut's neck. However, she bit back the words. Seeing Ben pat Red now, she knew that he hadn't meant to be cruel. He obviously just used very different methods from her – unfortunately the kind of forceful methods that most of the horse world used.

As far as Amy was concerned, she couldn't see why anyone would train with force when you could achieve just as much – more, even – through co-operation and understanding.

"There are other ways to get a horse to do what you want," she said to Ben. Clicking her tongue, she cantered Sundance in a circle.

"You're not really going to jump it, are you?" Ben called in surprise. "Isn't it a bit big for him?"

Ignoring him, Amy turned Sundance towards the tree. His ears pricked up, his stride lengthened confidently, and in one smooth leap they were over.

"Way to go!" Ben exclaimed, looking very impressed. "For a pony, he sure can jump!"

Amy nodded as she trotted over. "He's won Large Pony Hunter Champion three times now. But I don't get that much chance to compete him. I'd like to try a few junior jumper classes, though."

"You should," Ben said. "With a jump like that he should have a great chance."

Amy patted Sundance, pleased at Ben's approval. "We rescued him from going for meat," she said. "He was so bad-tempered no one could cope with him. Now there are loads of people that would like to buy him. But I'll never let him go."

"I know how you feel," Ben said. He stroked Red's shoulder. "I'd never sell Red either. No matter what anyone offered me."

Seeing Red turn and nuzzle Ben's hand, Amy began to forgive Ben for how he had behaved earlier. It was obvious that he loved Red deeply and that the horse adored him in return.

She smiled back at Ben and they continued along the track.

Ben patted Red. "I'm entered for a show next month with him. I thought I'd do a couple of classes to keep him going over the winter and then campaign him seriously next summer." He looked at Amy. "We could do some shows together. My trailer takes up to three horses. You could campaign Sundance too."

Amy was flattered but she shook her head. "Thanks, but I couldn't be away from Heartland for that long."

"What a waste," Ben said. "You could be really good."

Amy shrugged. "Heartland's more important to me than competing."

"Nothing's more important to me than competing," Ben said, his voice suddenly sounding determined. Shortening his reins, he leant forward in his saddle. "Come on, I'll race you to the bend in the track!"

Chapter Three

When Amy and Ben got back to Heartland, Ty was lunging Moochie. "We'd better start on the grooming," Amy said.

"Sure," Ben replied. "I'll be with you as soon as I've sorted Red out."

Amy thought that Ben meant he would just give Red a quick rub down; however, it was almost an hour before he eventually reappeared. "OK, who do you want me to start on?" he asked.

Amy was just finishing Jasmine. There were only three horses left to groom. "Can you do Jake and Sugarfoot?" she said, feeling slightly irritated that he had been so long.

Ben nodded cheerfully and fetched a grooming kit. When he came back, Amy was just going into Dancer's stall. "That's Dancer, isn't it?" Ben said.

Amy nodded.

Ben went to pat Dancer's neck, but he moved too quickly and the mare reacted like lightning. Throwing her head up, she snapped at Ben's arm.

"Hey!" Ben shouted, smacking her shoulder.

"Ben! No!" Amy cried in horror, grabbing his arm.

It was too late. Dancer bucked in fear.

"Get out!" Amy cried, yanking at Ben's arm.

She dragged him out of the stall and shut the door just as Dancer's hooves smashed into the back wall. Almost beside herself with anger, she turned on him. "How could you be so stupid!" she cried. "Dancer's scared enough of people as it is!"

Ben stared at her. "But she tried to bite me!"

"So? We *don't* hit horses here."

"You mean you just let them bite?" Ben exclaimed. "That's crazy! How will they ever learn to respect you if you let them get away with things like that?"

Amy's grey eyes flashed. "You don't need to hit a horse to get it to respect you. Particularly not a horse like Dancer who has been mistreated."

"So what *do* you do?" Ben said.

"Treat them with the respect they deserve, show them understanding, and let them realize that there is nothing to fear. Have you seen the scars on Dancer's head?" Amy demanded. "They were caused by having a halter on so tightly that her skin was rubbed raw. A halter that was kept on for over a year. Of course she tried to bite you when you put your hand up to her head like that. What would you have done if you had been her?"

Ben looked slightly shamefaced. "I didn't realize." He looked at the mare – now standing trembling at the back of her stall. "Hey, I'm sorry if I upset her."

Amy took a deep breath to try and control her anger. "Look, just make sure you remember that we never hit any of the horses here. Every single one of them is damaged in some way. What we need to do is gain their trust, not scare them even more."

Ben swallowed hard. "OK, I get it." He looked again at Dancer again. "Is there anything you can do to calm her down?"

"I'll see," Amy said. Leaving the halter on the floor, she walked quietly into the stall. Dancer stared at her warily.

"It's OK, girl," Amy told her softly, feeling in her pocket for the packet of mints and offering her one. "I won't hurt you."

Dancer watched Amy for a moment and then stepped forward cautiously, her neck outstretched, her brown and white nostrils blowing in and out. Amy let the mare snuffle the mint up from her hand and then moved quietly to stand beside her shoulder. Dancer shifted uneasily in the straw. Very gently, still speaking soothingly to the frightened horse, Amy put her hand lightly on Dancer's shoulder and began to move her fingers in a series of small circles, each circle moving on to a new patch of skin.

Forgetting about Ben watching from the doorway, she concentrated totally on the mare. As the minutes passed, she felt the horse's muscles begin to relax slightly, and Amy slowed the circles down, moving them gradually up Dancer's neck towards her head. She lightened her touch every time the mare tensed, but gradually Dancer started to relax more and more until she was allowing Amy to work tiny circles over her muzzle, nostrils and lips.

As Amy worked, the mare yawned and slowly lowered her head, her eyes half closing. At last Amy stopped and, moving quietly to the door, she picked up the halter and slipped it over Dancer's nose.

Dancer didn't even flinch. Buckling it up, Amy led the now calm mare towards the front of the stall.

"That's amazing," Ben said in surprise. "She's calmed down just because of a massage?"

"It's not really massage," Amy explained. "It's a form of therapy called T-Touch." She tied Dancer up. "You see, you don't need to use force to get a horse to do what you want."

Ben frowned. "I get your point with horses like Dancer," he said. "But a regular horse – well, they respond to discipline. Look at Red. I'm firm with him but you can't say that he's scared of me, and he works great."

"But why use force when you can get a horse to work just as well for you without it?" Amy said.

Ben shrugged. "It's just how I learnt to do it." He saw her face. "Look, it works for me. But don't worry, I'll respect your rules with Heartland's horses." He picked up the grooming kit again. "Now, I'd better get on with grooming that Shetland – Sugarfoot, you said his name was?"

Amy nodded and started to brush Dancer. She didn't know quite what to make of Ben. He seemed so sceptical, not at all prepared to take their ideas on board, and yet he was such a good rider and obviously devoted to Red. Surely, with Ben's natural ability, over time she and Ty would be able to persuade him to change his ideas. She patted Dancer. She hoped so.

At five o'clock, Amy and Ty started to fill the evening hay nets. They were running late as usual. "At least all the horses have been exercised," Amy said to Ty as they stuffed sweet-smelling meadow hay into the nets.

"Yeah, and with three of us we should be able to get the rest of the tack finished in no time," Ty said. "That's if we all put our backs into it."

Just then, there was the sound of footsteps. Ben looked over the door. "OK, then. I'm going."

Amy stared at him. "Going? But the horses haven't been fed yet."

"But I only work until five," Ben said in surprise.

Amy was lost for words. He was right, of course. However, working with horses wasn't like a regular job; you didn't just leave when your hours were up.

"I normally stay until things are finished," Ty said pointedly.

"Great," Ben said cheerfully. "If you're staying, I'm OK to go then?"

"Well, actually, Ben, if you could stay until the feeds are done, it would be a help," Amy said quickly, seeing that he hadn't taken the hint.

Ben looked taken aback. "I guess I could."

"Good," Amy said, feeling awkward that she had to ask. "In that case, if you want to start mixing the feeds and we'll finish these nets off."

Ben did as he was asked. As they heard the rattle of the buckets being put out on the floor, Amy and Ty exchanged glances. They continued filling the hay nets in silence.

At last the horses were fed. "See you, then," Ben said.

Amy nodded, not able to bring herself to say that the tack still needed cleaning.

She watched Ben drive off. "Well," she said to Ty. "What do you think of *that*?"

"I guess he's used to his aunt's barn where there's enough staff for working hours to be kept to quite strictly," Ty said.

Amy thought about Lisa Stillman's immaculate stud with its army of stable-hands and nodded. "It must be a big change for him. He's probably not even used to mucking out and doing things like that."

Ty looked at her. "Do you think he'll ever fit in here, Amy?"

Amy remembered her own doubts earlier in the afternoon. "I'm sure he will," she said, trying to be positive. "He just needs time to adjust."

For a moment, Ty didn't say anything, but then he nodded. "Well, we'll just have to wait and see."

Ben didn't arrive the next morning until Amy was going into the house to get changed for school. She didn't have time to think about his lateness. School mornings were always hectic and as usual she hadn't got any of her things ready. She showered in about two minutes flat, pulled on some clean clothes and raced downstairs.

"What about breakfast, Amy!" her grandpa said despairingly, as she grabbed her trainers.

"I haven't got time!" Amy said. "I'll be late for the bus!" She slung her rucksack over her shoulder.

"But Amy, you can't go without breakfast," Jack Bartlett said.

"Why do we have to go through this every morning?" Lou said from the kitchen table. "I don't see why it's so hard to get yourself a bit more organized, Amy."

"Here, take this," her grandpa said, pushing a muffin into Amy's hand.

"Thanks, Grandpa!" Amy said, giving him a kiss. "See you later. Bye, Lou!"

With that she ran out of the house.

Ty was standing by the tap, filling up a water bucket. "Have a good day," he called.

"Like *that*'s likely," Amy said, pausing briefly. "I've got double maths first thing."

Ty grinned. "Rather you than me."

"See you later!" said Amy, jogging off down the drive.

She made it to the stop just as the bus arrived. Soraya had saved a seat beside her. "So, come on – tell me all the gossip about Ben," she said as Amy sat down.

"Well, he's not very good at being on time," Amy said. "He's been late both mornings since he got here."

"And you're *never* late," Soraya grinned, looking at Amy's flushed face and dishevelled hair.

Amy grinned back. "OK, OK."

"Did you find out whether he's got a girlfriend?" Soraya asked.

"Yes," Amy said. "And he hasn't."

"Now *that* really is interesting," Soraya said slowly. "So, how's he fitting in at Heartland?"

As Amy started to tell her all about Ben, she noticed that the girl sitting in a seat across the aisle kept looking at her. "Who's that?" Amy said to Soraya, when the girl looked away.

"I don't know," Soraya replied. "Maybe she's new."

The girl glanced at them again. She had short brown hair and a heart-shaped face.

"Hi," Soraya said, smiling at her in her usual friendly way.

The girl went red. "Oh ... hi," she said nervously.

"Are you new around here?" Soraya asked, leaning forward.

The girl nodded. "Yes. My name's Claire Whitely."

"We thought we hadn't seen you before," Soraya said. "Where have you moved from?"

"Philadelphia," the girl said. "We're here because of my mom's job."

"Well, I'm Soraya Martin and this is Amy Fleming," Soraya told her. "If you want to know anything about school, just ask us."

Amy nodded.

"Thanks," Claire said. Her cheeks went a bit pinker. "Actually, I couldn't help overhearing your conversation," she said, looking at Amy. "Do you . . . do you live at Heartland?"

"Yeah," Amy replied, feeling surprised.

Claire's blue eyes widened. "I read about Heartland in an issue of *Horse Life*. It sounds amazing. I knew it was somewhere in North-Eastern Virginia but I didn't know it was here."

"Do you ride?" Amy asked her.

"Yeah," Claire said shyly. "My dad's just bought me my own horse. Him and my mom are divorced and he's just left to go and work in Europe for a few months. My horse is a Thoroughbred called Flint."

"Cool!" Soraya said.

Claire nodded. "I've been wanting a horse for ages, and with me not seeing Daddy much, he said that I could have one. Flint's brilliant. He was really expensive, but he's won loads, so he must be worth the money."

Looking at the glow in Claire's eyes as she talked about

Flint, Amy forgave her for boasting a bit. She obviously adored her horse.

Claire looked at her and swallowed. "Would you ... would you like to come and see him?" she asked hesitantly. "You too, Soraya. How about after school today? But don't feel that you have to... I mean, if you're busy or whatever," she added hurriedly.

"I'd like to see him," Amy said.

"Me too," Soraya said

"You would?" Claire looked as if she couldn't believe it.

Amy nodded. "Where do you keep him?"

"Green Briar," Claire replied eagerly. "Do you know it?"

Amy and Soraya's eyes met. They knew it all too well. Green Briar was a large hunter/jumper barn that specialized in producing push-button horses and ponies who would always be in the ribbons. It was run by Val Grant. Her daughter, Ashley, was in the same class as Amy and Soraya at school, and whenever Amy took Sundance in the show ring, she was one of Amy's fiercest rivals.

"We sure do," Soraya replied dryly.

"Great," Claire said, oblivious to the look that had passed between them. "Do you want to come after school, then?"

"I'll have to go home first and check everything's OK," Amy said. "But we could meet you there?" She didn't particularly want to go to Green Briar, but she guessed there was no way out, and it would be interesting to check out Flint.

"OK," Claire said, her eyes shining. "That would be great."

* * *

School seemed to drag by that day. All Amy could think about was how Ben was getting on with Ty at home and going to see Claire's horse. Soraya phoned her mom at lunchtime and Mrs Martin agreed to give them a lift over to Green Briar.

"See you later," Amy said to Soraya and Claire, as she got off the bus.

"Yeah – bye," they called.

Amy hurried up Heartland's winding drive. When she reached the top, she saw Ty coming out of the tack-room. "Hi," she said, going over to him. "How's today been?"

"Hectic," Ty said. "But most of the horses have been worked. There's just Ivy and Solo left."

"I'll do them," Amy offered. "But do you mind if I go over to Green Briar first?"

"Green Briar?" Ty echoed. "What do you want to go there for?"

Amy explained about Flint. "I'd like to see him, and Soraya's mom has said that she'll drive us. I won't be long."

"Fine," Ty said. "I'll get Ben to give me a hand sweeping the yard – when he's finished riding Red."

"He's riding Red?" Amy said, surprised that Ben should be riding his own horse when there was still yard work to be done.

Ty nodded. "Yeah. He rode him for an hour this morning as well." He looked concerned. "Don't you think being ridden twice in one day is quite a lot of work for a young horse?"

"Ben did tell me that he's got a show coming up next month," Amy said. "And lots of competition horses get ridden twice a day."

"Yeah, but they don't normally get jumped for an hour each time," Ty said. "I could understand him riding once in the ring and once out on the trails but Ben's ridden both times in the ring."

Amy frowned. Ty was right. Two training sessions, each an hour long, was a lot of work for any horse, let alone a young horse like Red.

"And I could have done with a bit more help," Ty added.

Amy nodded. "Maybe we should speak to him later."

She went to get changed. As she came out of the house, Ben brought Red down from the training ring. "Hi!" he called, catching sight of her and stopping Red. "He's been great today."

Amy didn't know what to say. She wanted to tackle him about jumping Red twice in a day and ask him why he hadn't helped Ty more, but didn't know quite how to start. It was a tricky situation because his aunt was paying for him to be there. Under other circumstances she wouldn't have hesitated to speak out, but this was different.

"Good," she said. "I ... er, think Ty could use a hand with the yard."

"Sure," Ben said. "I'll just cool Red down first."

"OK, but don't be too long," Amy said sharply.

Ben looked surprised.

Just then, the Martins' car came up the drive and Amy realized that the conversation would have to wait.

"Hi, Ben," Soraya said, getting out of the car.

Ben smiled at her. "Hi, there."

Seeing that Soraya looked as if she was about to start a conversation, Amy grabbed her arm. They didn't want to be late for Claire. "Hello, Mrs Martin," she said, as she pulled Soraya into the back of the car.

"Hi, Amy," Mrs Martin replied, turning the car around.

"Did you see the way Ben smiled at me?" Soraya said dreamily to her. "He is *so* cute!"

"Soraya Martin!" her mom said, overhearing. "I thought you liked going to Heartland because of the horses."

"I do!" Soraya protested.

But then, shooting Amy a sideways look that her mom couldn't see, she grinned.

Amy smiled back at her friend, but inwardly she still felt troubled by the situation she had just had to deal with.

Claire was waiting for them in the smart car park at Green Briar. "Flint's stall is in that barn there," she said, leading them across the immaculate yard towards a spacious modern barn. They passed a large all-weather training ring where three beautiful horses were being schooled over a line of fences. In the middle of the ring stood Val Grant. With a cell-phone clipped on to the back of her tight maroon breeches, she shouted out instructions to the riders. Amy hurried past, not wanting to be seen. If she could see Flint and get away from Green Briar without having to talk to Val Grant or her daughter, Ashley, then so much the better. She cringed as there was a rattle of poles and she heard Val Grant's voice yell out in strident tones. "What do you think your stick's for, Yvonne? Use it!"

Amy exchanged looks with Soraya and they hurried into the barn.

"That's him," Claire said. "Just there – five stalls down on the left. The dark grey."

Amy looked down the row of stalls to where a beautiful iron-grey Thoroughbred was looking over his half-door. His elegant ears were pricked, his brown eyes were large and thoughtful.

"He's very handsome," Amy said, going over. "Hi, boy."

Flint looked at her rather aloofly.

Amy peered over the stall door. He was a fantastic-looking horse, very athletic with clean and strong legs and a noble head.

Soraya and Claire joined her. "He's a looker, isn't he?" Claire said, waiting for their approval.

"He sure is," Soraya said.

Amy nodded in agreement. "Are you going to ride him?" she asked.

Claire seemed suddenly hesitant. "Um ... well ... I don't know."

"Oh, you've got to!" Soraya said.

"OK," Claire agreed slowly. "I'll get his tack."

A few minutes later, Claire returned with Flint's saddle and bridle. Her fingers fumbled with the bolt as she let herself into the stall. As she moved towards Flint, he tossed his head into the air.

"Steady, boy," Claire said, her voice sounding nervous.

Flint side-stepped away from her and moved to the back of his stall so that his hindquarters were pointing in Claire's direction. Putting his ears back, Flint lifted one back hoof and stamped it on the ground. Claire jumped back quickly.

"Is he always like this?" Soraya asked.

"Not always, but most of the time," Claire said, seeming grateful for the excuse to step back to the door. "He was OK at first, but he's been getting worse. Sometimes it can take me twenty minutes to tack up."

Amy stared at her in astonishment. "Twenty minutes!"

"He just keeps lifting his back foot at me like that," Claire said, her face going red. "I'm not sure what to do."

Amy frowned. She had seen the way Flint had been watching Claire as he stood in the corner, his ears pricked, his eyes bright. He didn't look mean. In fact, she had a strong feeling that he was just taking advantage of Claire's lack of experience. "Here, do you want me to have a go?" she said.

Claire gratefully handed her the bridle.

Ignoring the way Flint lifted his back hoof up from the floor, Amy marched round to his head, grabbed his mane so that he couldn't swing away and deftly slipped the reins over his head. "Got you!" she said, taking hold of his nose and pulling the head-piece over his ears. Flint looked at her determined face and didn't object.

"I think you're going to have to be a bit firmer with him," she said to Claire. "He's just being naughty."

She finished tacking Flint up and then led him outside and handed the reins to Claire.

Claire glanced at the main training ring. Val Grant was still working with the three riders. "We'll take him to the back ring," she said quickly.

Amy and Soraya followed her round to a smaller training ring behind the barns. Claire led Flint in through the gate and then mounted.

As soon as she was in the saddle, Flint started to side-step. "Steady," Claire said, her hands grabbing at the reins. Looking at Amy and Soraya she tried to smile. "I'll just walk and trot him for a bit," she said.

As she rode off, Soraya turned to Amy. "She doesn't seem very confident," she said.

"I know," Amy said in a low voice as Flint jogged around the school. Although Claire's position in the saddle was basically good, she was stiff and tense. "And he's quite a handful."

As they watched, Flint began to settle down and Claire seemed to relax. But she didn't canter him.

After a bit, she rode Flint over to the gate. "He's great, isn't he?" she said proudly.

"Yeah," Amy agreed.

"But he does look a bit lively," Soraya said.

"That horse just needs someone on its back who can ride," a voice said behind them.

Amy swung round. Ashley Grant was standing there, arms crossed, platinum-blonde hair falling on to her shoulders.

"I've told you, Flint's totally the wrong horse for a novice like *you*," Ashley said to Claire. She shrugged. "But if you want, I guess I could spare the time to ride him."

"Thanks, but I think I'll bring him in now," Claire said quickly. She hurriedly started to dismount. "He's done enough."

Ashley laughed and turned to Amy. "So how's business at ... Heartland?" she said, her eyebrows raising in an irritatingly mocking way as she said Heartland's name.

"Extremely busy, actually," Amy said coldly, moving to open the gate for Claire. "All our stalls are full and we've got a new stable-hand."

Ashley looked surprised. "What's happened to Ty?"

"As *well* as Ty," Amy said as Claire led Flint out of the ring.

Ashley crossed her arms. "You're never going to keep Ty, you know. He's good – even Mom says so. He could go places."

"He could, but he doesn't want to," Amy said.

"I wouldn't be so sure, if I were you." Ashley said. "Does he know that we've just started looking for a new head-groom? He might want to apply."

Amy laughed incredulously. "Get real, Ashley. Ty would never want to come and work somewhere like *here*."

Ashley looked round at the immaculate yard. "Oh really? So Ty wouldn't want to work on a yard with three training rings, a cross-country course, three barns, efficient staff and top-quality horses? No, of course, Amy," she said sarcastically, "working here is every stable-hand's nightmare. Particularly when you think of what Ty can have instead – one run-down yard with a single barn, two small rings and a selection of horses that no one wants."

Amy longed to say something clever back, but the truth in Ashley's words hit home. "Ty wouldn't come here!" she said, wanting desperately to reassure herself.

"Mom would pay a lot to get someone like him," Ashley said. "Maybe I'll tell her to give him a call," she added casually.

"You can do what you like!" Amy exclaimed, feeling her temper start to rise. "But Ty won't leave Heartland!"

Ashley's lips curved into an irritating smile. "Really?" she said. Her green eyes challenged Amy. "Well, I guess we'll just have to see about that."

Chapter Four

Amy was still angry with Ashley when Mrs Martin dropped her back at Heartland half an hour later. She was sure that Ty wouldn't leave Heartland. But how much would Val Grant offer him? Whatever it was, Amy knew that Lou would never be able to match it. And what about the opportunities available to him? Green Briar was four times as big as Heartland.

She pushed away her doubts. She was being ridiculous. Ty loved Heartland. She should know him better than to think he would ever consider leaving.

As she walked up the yard she saw Ben coming out of Red's stall. "Hi," he said.

Amy remembered that she had been planning to talk to him some more. She went over, wondering how to begin. "He's in great condition," she said, patting Red's muscular neck.

Ben nodded. "Yeah. I ride him twice a day."

"Isn't that a bit much for a young horse?" Amy said, trying to get the conversation round to what she wanted to talk about.

Ben shook his head. "If I want to make it to the top he needs to be fit."

"Yeah, but you don't need to school him twice a day," Amy said. "Ty said you rode him twice in the ring today. He was a bit concerned."

"What does he know?" Ben said, looking angry. "He doesn't even ride competitively."

"He knows a lot!" Amy said, jumping to Ty's defence. "And he only mentioned it because he was worried about Red."

"Well, I don't need him to look out for my horse!" Ben said. "I decide what's best for Red." He looked at her. "You should appreciate the demands of training a top competition horse, Amy. You saw your mom and dad do it."

Amy didn't want to get into a huge fight with Ben on only his second day. "I guess," she said, reluctantly backing down. Presumably he had done the same at Fairfield and Lisa Stillman had thought it reasonable training for a competing horse.

Just then the phone rang. "I'll get it!" Ty said, coming out of the tack-room.

Five minutes later, he walked back up the yard. Amy was filling Jake's water bucket. "Who was it?" she called.

Ty walked towards her, his dark eyes amused. "You will *never* guess."

"I have no idea," Amy said, shaking her head.

"It was Val Grant," Ty said. "And she's just offered me a job at Green Briar." He had a huge grin on his face.

Amy was stunned. "Val Grant!"

Ty took in her expression and burst out laughing. "Like I'd really say yes! Though she did offer me twice the salary that I get here *and* I'd get to be head-groom. You know," he said, mock-seriously, "maybe I *should* have considered it, after all."

"Ty!" Amy exclaimed, relieved that he didn't seem to be taking the job offer seriously, but worried that he was even slightly tempted.

"I mean I'd get the chance to work with a huge number of different horses, to travel, to make a name for myself..." Ty teased.

"And best of all, you'd get to work with Val Grant!" Amy put in.

"You're right." Ty grimaced. "And no money's worth that!"

That night, as the family sat down to dinner, Lou asked how Ben was settling in.

Amy didn't know what to say.

"There isn't a problem, is there, Amy?" Grandpa said, seeing her hesitate.

"No ... no, he's OK," Amy said, reaching out for the water jug.

Jack Bartlett frowned. "Just OK?" Amy could tell that he thought she was trying to hide something. "Amy, what's on your mind?"

"Nothing." Amy saw her grandpa's eyebrows raise. "It's just he's got slightly different ideas than we have," she tried to explain. "But I'm sure it's not going to be a major problem."

At that moment, the phone rang.

"I'll answer it!" Amy said, glad of the distraction. She jumped up and grabbed the receiver. "Heartland – Amy Fleming speaking."

"Hi, Amy. It's Scott."

Hearing the familiar voice of their local vet, Amy smiled. "Hi, Scott."

Scott cleared his throat. "Is Lou there?" he asked.

"Yeah," Amy said, nodding. "I'll just pass you over." She held the cordless phone out to her sister. "It's Scott," she said, grinning.

Lou's face went pink. "For me?"

"Yes," Amy replied, her eyes glinting teasingly at her. "For you."

Lou took the phone. "Hi, Scott," she said, walking away from the table and turning her back on Amy. "Yes, I'm fine. How are you?"

Amy grinned at their grandpa as she sat back down, forgetting the conversation about Ben. "Scott's going to ask Lou out on a date!" she said.

Jack Bartlett shook his head, but Amy saw him smile as he

looked away. Although Grandpa would never say anything, she knew that he would be just as pleased as her if Scott and Lou were to start dating. For the last couple of months – ever since Lou had dumped her last boyfriend – she had been becoming increasingly friendly with Scott. But so far nothing had happened. However, this was the first time that Scott had rung just to speak to Lou.

Amy turned hopefully in her chair. She could just hear what Lou was saying. "I'd love to, Scott! That sounds great. OK, I'll see you then."

"Well?" Amy demanded, as Lou put the phone down. "Did he ask you out on a date?"

"Yes," Lou said, turning round and looking stunned. "He did. We're going out on Saturday."

"Oh, Lou! That's brilliant!" Amy cried, jumping to her feet and hugging her sister. "You and Scott are totally perfect for each other."

"It's only one date, Amy," Lou laughed, but despite her practical words her blue eyes sparkled.

The next day on the school bus, Amy told Soraya the news. "Isn't it brilliant?" she said.

"I wonder if Matt knows," Soraya said.

Matt was one of their best friends and Scott's younger brother. As soon as he got on the bus they told him.

"Cool," he said. He looked hopefully at Amy. "You know, we could always see if they want to make it a double date?"

"Like they'll want us there as well," Amy said.

"We could go somewhere else," Matt said.

"Maybe another time," Amy said.

Matt sighed theatrically. "Rejected again."

Amy grinned at him. "You'll get over it." Matt had been trying to persuade her to go out with him for almost a year now, but somehow she just couldn't see him as a boyfriend. She caught Soraya looking at her. She knew Soraya thought she was crazy to keep turning Matt down. He was cute, intelligent, popular and great fun to be around.

"So who's the new girl you were talking to yesterday?" Matt said, glancing along the bus to where Claire was sitting.

"Claire Whitely," Amy replied.

"She's just moved here from Philadelphia," Soraya said. "We went to see her horse yesterday. She's keeping it at Green Briar."

"How's she getting on with Ashley?" Matt said.

"She seemed a bit in awe of her," Amy said, remembering the way Claire had stammered and gone red when Ashley had spoken to her.

"I don't blame her," Matt joked. "Ashley's enough to scare anyone."

Amy smiled. "Well, I guess Claire's just going to have to learn to stand up to her – if she's going to carry on keeping Flint at Green Briar, anyway."

"Poor thing," Soraya said with feeling. "It's bad enough seeing Ashley at school every day – imagine having to see her afterwards as well." She nodded towards the front of the bus. "You know, she doesn't seem too happy today. I've been watching her."

Amy looked to the front of the bus where Claire was sitting. She was hugging her bag, obviously lost in thought.

When they arrived at school, Amy pushed forward to catch up with Claire as she got off the bus. "Hi. How are you?" she asked.

"Fine," Claire said quickly. Just then, Matt and a group of his friends jumped off the bus and pushed past them. One of them knocked against Claire's arm with his bag. "Ow!" she gasped, clutching her arm.

"What's up?" Amy demanded.

Claire bit her lip. She looked like she was struggling not to cry.

"Are you OK?" Soraya said, joining them and glancing at Claire holding her arm. "What's wrong?"

"It's my arm," Claire said. She moved to one side to let the rest of the students get by, and then shrugged off her jacket. She was wearing a long-sleeved T-shirt underneath. When she rolled up the sleeve both Amy and Soraya gasped. On her upper arm there was a massive bruise. Black and deep-purple, it radiated out from a pale imprint of teeth-marks in the centre.

"What happened?" Soraya asked.

Claire swallowed and pulled her jacket back on. "It was Flint," she said. "He bit me last night after you'd gone."

"What did your mom say?" Amy asked.

"I haven't told her," Claire said. "And the worst thing is that she's coming to watch me ride tonight. If he bites me when she's there, she'll want to get rid of him." Her eyes filled with tears. "She didn't think much of Daddy buying him in the first place. She says I'm too inexperienced to own a horse of my own."

Soraya glanced at Amy. "Maybe Amy could help. She's good with aggressive horses."

"Could you?" Claire said, hope lighting up her eyes as she looked at Amy.

Amy didn't know what to say. "Well, there's not much I can do while he's at Green Briar. You see, Val Grant's the trainer there and she'd go crazy if I came over and started helping you." She saw Claire's face start to crumple and felt bad. "But I can give you some advice on how to deal with him. And maybe I could come and help you tack him up tonight so that your mom doesn't see him being aggressive. It's not going to solve the problem, but at least it will give you a bit more time."

Claire nodded. "Please do. If I can just stop Mom finding out, I'll work with him – I'll do whatever you say. I'm sure he'll get better."

"OK, that's settled then. I'll come down straight after school." Amy spoke lightly, but deep down she was worried. It was one thing for her to tell Claire what to do about Flint, but quite another for Claire to carry out her instructions.

From what Amy had seen of Flint, it was clear that he needed an experienced rider – and nothing she could *say* was going to turn Claire into that.

When she got back to Heartland after school, Amy persuaded Grandpa to drive her over to Green Briar. "I'll be back to collect you in an hour," he said, as he dropped her outside the smart white gates.

"OK, thanks. See you later," Amy replied. As she walked through the gates, she saw Claire hurrying towards her. "Thank goodness you're here. Mom's going to be here in about twenty minutes," she panted as she reached Amy. "And we've got to get him groomed and tacked up before then. But I warn you, he's behaving really badly."

Claire had already carried her grooming kit around to Flint's stall. As she opened the door, he threw his head up and pinned his ears back. Claire hesitated. "There's a good boy," she said nervously. Flint stamped the ground and swished his tail. "That's what he was doing yesterday," Claire told Amy. She took a cautious step towards the horse. "Here, boy."

Flint swung his teeth at her and Claire jumped back with a gasp.

Amy took charge. She pushed past Claire. "That's enough!" she said sharply to Flint. He looked at her, his head held high, his eyes seeming to weigh her up.

Amy took the halter from Claire and moved in swiftly

beside Flint's head. In one quick movement, she slipped the halter over his nose and flicked the head-piece over his poll. As she went to buckle it up, he tossed his head up. "No!" she said. Flint looked at her and gave in.

Amy patted his neck and looked thoughtfully at his head. Her mom had always said that a horse's personality was stamped on its face. Flint had a slight moose nose, large eyes and large, open nostrils. All of these attributes suggested that he was a highly intelligent horse. Amy looked at his ears. They were long and narrow – the sort of ears that were often found with horses who were difficult and temperamental. *Highly intelligent, but difficult and temperamental*, Amy thought as she stroked Flint's straight nose. *Totally the wrong horse for a novice rider*.

Amy's mom had taught her that most horses who were aggressive acted that way because they were scared. However, Amy was inclined to believe that Flint was one of the exceptions to this rule. She had a strong feeling that he was being aggressive with Claire simply because he thought he could get away with it. *And he's right*, she thought.

"What can I do with him, Amy?" Claire asked.

"You're just going to have to be firm," Amy said. She saw Claire's face. "I don't mean hit him – just tell him off when he misbehaves and try not to be nervous." She began to tie Flint up. "We should get moving. Your mom will be here soon."

At first, when Claire tried to help with the grooming Flint swished his tail, but a firm word from Amy soon stopped his display of bad manners. "You've just got to let him know that you're in charge," she said.

At last, Flint was ready. They saddled him up and led to the small training ring. As Claire put her foot in the stirrup, Flint danced on the spot. Claire tightened the reins nervously. "Stand." She tried to sound firm but it didn't work. Her voice was too high. Flint side-stepped. Giving up trying to get him to stand still, Claire mounted.

Flint jogged around the ring. After one circuit, Claire let him trot. He pulled impatiently at the bit, his hindquarters sidling inwards.

Suddenly Flint caught sight of a pile of jumps stacked behind the fence. He spooked violently. The sudden movement took Claire by surprise and she lost a stirrup and half dropped her reins. Feeling the grip on his reins loosen, Flint put his head down and bucked three times.

"Hang on, Claire!" Amy cried from the gate.

Claire stayed on for the first buck, but as Flint's head went down between his knees for the second time, she lost her other stirrup and landed on his neck. The third buck sent her flying over his shoulder and she crashed to the floor.

"Claire!" Amy exclaimed, her heart pounding as she scrambled over the gate.

Her voice was drowned out by a scream from behind her. "Oh my goodness! *Claire!*"

Amy swung round. A woman with shoulder-length brown hair was running towards the gate.

"Mom!"

Amy looked back at Claire. She was sitting up, looking at the woman with horror in her eyes.

Chapter Five

Amy didn't stop. She ran to the centre of the ring. "Are you OK?" she demanded, reaching Claire.

To her relief, Claire nodded. "Yeah, I think so." Her voice trembled as she watched her mom opening the gate. "I've totally blown it now, Amy. I can't believe Mom saw me fall off!"

"I'll get Flint," Amy said.

"Claire!" Mrs Whitely cried, her voice high.

"I'm OK, Mom," Claire said, getting up and walking slowly towards her.

Amy went to catch Flint. He was grazing nonchalantly on a patch of grass at the side of the ring. As Amy approached, he looked up at her, his muscles visibly tensing beneath his coat.

Amy pulled out a packet of mints from her pocket and held one out to him. "Here, boy," she said calmly.

She stood still and waited. Flint gazed at her for a moment longer and then the lure of the mint became too strong for him. Stretching out his muzzle he walked over to her.

"Good boy," Amy said, quietly taking hold of his reins.

As Flint crunched on the mint, he regarded her with his intelligent dark eyes.

Amy shook her head. "Now, Flint, that wasn't the thing to do." She patted his iron-grey shoulder. Flint might be naughty but she liked him. He was young and full of spirit.

She glanced over to the gate. Claire and her mom seemed to be arguing. "Looks like it's time to face the music," Amy said to Flint, her heart sinking. Clicking her tongue, she led him on.

"He'll have to go, Claire!" she heard Mrs Whitely saying as she got near. "He's dangerous. Anyone can see that. Your father was a fool getting you a horse like that."

"He's not dangerous, Mom!" Claire exclaimed. "He's just lively."

"Lively? He's going to break your neck!"

"I promise you, Mom, he's not!" Claire protested, turning to Amy for support. "Please tell her, Amy."

"He's just high-spirited," Amy said quickly. She saw the shock and concern on Mrs Whitely's face and stepped forward, holding out her hand. "I'm Amy Fleming. My sister and I run Heartland, a rescue centre for neglected and problem horses."

"I told you about Amy, Mom," Claire put in.

Mrs Whitely nodded distractedly. "Yes ... yes, I remember. Pleased to meet you, Amy." She looked back at Claire. "Oh, sweetheart," she said, shaking her head. "I just don't know what to do. I can't let you carry on riding him if he's going to buck like that. I won't sleep at night."

"But, Mom...!" Claire protested.

"Maybe Claire could get some help with him," Amy broke in. "Have some lessons. He's really not dangerous, Mrs Whitely. Claire just needs to learn to be firmer."

"Maybe," Mrs Whitely sighed. She looked at Flint. "I guess I could ask Val Grant if she would help."

"No!" Claire interrupted. "Not Val Grant. She'll make me hit him. I want Amy to help."

"I told you, I can't – not while he's here," Amy said. "Val Grant wouldn't allow it."

"Then we'll move him to Heartland," Claire said. "Won't we, Mom?"

Amy stared in surprise.

"Claire!" Mrs Whitely exclaimed quickly. "You can't just make a decision like that."

"Why not?" Claire said. "I don't like it here. Ashley Grant's a bully and she's always making fun of me. And Flint's really good with Amy. She can teach me what to do." She turned to Amy. "You will help, won't you?"

"But all our stalls are full at the moment," Amy said. She saw Claire's face fall. Was there a way she could help? She desperately wanted to. "I guess as it's still quite warm," she said, thinking fast, "my own pony, Sundance, could live out full-time. If it's just for a few weeks, it won't hurt him – and then Flint could have his stall."

Mrs Whitely looked as if she didn't know what to say. "Well, that's very kind of you…" she began.

"Say yes, Mom!" Claire begged her. "I'll do anything – just please say yes."

Mrs Whitely shrugged helplessly. "OK then," she said at last. "If Amy thinks she can help, then I'll give him a second chance. But just for a month. If he's no better by then, he has to go, Claire."

"He will be better," Claire said. "I just know he will!"

When Amy got back to Heartland, she found Lou and her grandpa doing the accounts in the kitchen. She told them about Flint. "He can have Sundance's stall," she explained. "Sundance can live out in the field for a bit."

Grandpa nodded. "It won't hurt him, and it sounds like this friend of yours could use some help."

"When's the horse arriving?" Lou asked, opening the yard diary so that she could write Flint's arrival in.

"Mrs Whitely said she'd try and arrange to hire a trailer for Saturday," Amy said.

"I could take ours over to collect him," Grandpa said. "I haven't got anything else planned."

"Great!" Amy said. "I'll call Claire's mom and let her know."

"Have you told Ty?" Lou asked.

"No. Do you know where he is?" Amy asked.

"In the tack-room, I think," Lou said.

Amy hurried up to the tack-room. Ty was cleaning a saddle. She told him about Flint. "Her mom's said she'll give him a month. If he's not improving by that time she's going to sell him."

"Sounds like it's a case of the wrong horse with the wrong rider," Ty said.

Amy nodded. "Yeah, but Claire's desperate to keep him. And he's a fantastic horse. We've got to try and help. If Claire can just learn to be firmer with him then he'll start to respect her and stop behaving badly."

"It might take more than a month," Ty said, replacing the saddle on its rack.

"No, it won't," Amy said optimistically. "He's fine with me."

"But you've been around horses all your life," Ty said. "You just can't teach someone that kind of experience; it only comes with time."

Amy shrugged off his concerns. "It'll work out, you'll see." She changed the subject. "So where's Ben?"

"Guess," Ty said dryly.

"With Red?" Amy said, her heart sinking.

Ty nodded. "He's riding him up in the ring – for the second time. You know, he's probably only done about two hours' yard-work today. If I ask him to do something, he does it – but if I don't, he just hangs around in the tack-room or Red's stall. Half the time, it's just easier to do the job myself rather than to waste time tracking him down. I've tried saying something to him, but it didn't make a difference."

"Do you want me to talk to him again?" Amy offered.

Ty shrugged. "We could get Lou to – he might listen to her."

"Let me try first," Amy said. Somehow involving Lou made it seem like an official complaint, and she was still hoping that Ben was just taking time to settle in.

"OK," Ty said. "Good luck."

As Amy walked up to the schooling ring, she wondered what she was going to say.

Ben was cantering Red around the ring. Along one side he had set up a line of fences. As Amy reached the gate he turned Red towards them.

Amy frowned. Red's neck and shoulders were drenched with sweat. Seeing the jumps, Red threw his head high and plunged sideways. Ben pulled Red into a tight circle.

Amy stopped and watched. Red was fighting against Ben's control. He looked totally wound up.

Again, Ben turned him towards the fences and again Red plunged excitedly forward.

"No!" Ben shouted, yanking at Red's mouth.

Amy flinched as she saw Red throw his head up.

Ben turned Red into a tight circle again, his legs and seat

driving the horse forward, demanding obedience and submission. Amy knew that he was trying to stop Red from rushing too fast into the fences – but the firmer he got, the more excited Red became.

Amy forgot that she had come to talk to Ben about work. She ran to the gate. "Give him a break, Ben! Can't you see you're winding him up even more?"

Ben pulled Red into a halt and swung round in the saddle. "What?" he demanded.

His eyes looked angry, but Amy took no notice. "You're winding him up by making him canter in small circles like that!" she exclaimed.

"He has to learn!" Ben said. "The show's in three weeks."

"He's not going to learn while he's stressed," Amy protested. "Look, just take him out on the trails and let him cool off a bit. You can try again tomorrow."

Ben shook his head stubbornly. "I'm not giving in to him. He's going to learn *now*."

Red snorted and side-stepped. Shortening his reins again, Ben pushed him into a canter.

"Ben!" Amy exclaimed beginning to fee her temper rising.

But Ben took no notice. He cantered Red in a circle, ignoring Amy's protestations. Other than throwing herself in front of the horse, there was nothing Amy could do except watch.

To her relief, however, she realized that the moment's halt at the gate had calmed Red down slightly. Instead of fighting

Ben, he was now cantering smoothly, lowering his head and softening his jaw.

Ben turned him into the line of jumps. Amy held her breath.

"Go on, boy!" she whispered, as Red approached the fences with his ears pricked, but in a much calmer state of mind. Ben let him go, his stride lengthened and they flew over all three.

At the far end of the ring, Ben pulled him up. "Good boy!" he exclaimed, patting him hard.

He rode Red down the ring towards Amy. The stubborn, angry look had vanished from his eyes.

"See!" he said triumphantly as he got close. "That was way better! *Now* I'll take him out for a trail ride. You should never give in to a horse, Amy," he said as she opened the gate for him. "They have to learn to do what you want when you want. If they don't learn that, then you'll never have complete control. And that's what you need if you're going to make it to the top."

With that, he rode Red out of the gate and headed up towards the woods. "See you later."

For once lost for words, Amy watched him go. Although he had succeeded with Red using his techniques, there was no way she could agree with him. What was the point in having complete control if the horse didn't want to work for you? Surely far more could be achieved when a rider formed a partnership with the horse. And if that meant sometimes giving in to the horse, or accepting that the horse was a living, breathing creature who was going to have off-days just like humans did, then so be it. As far as she was concerned, it was a small price to pay to have a horse who loved his work and who would try, heart and soul, to please you.

She walked slowly down the yard. Like a lot of competitive horsey people, Ben clearly didn't share her beliefs. But then, she didn't have to put up with seeing those other people riding their horses every day. It really bothered her watching a horse being trained in this manner at Heartland.

"Did you talk to him?" Ty asked, appearing from the tack-room. "Is he going to bring Red in and start helping?"

Amy suddenly remembered that she had gone up to the training ring to talk to Ben about work. "I ... I didn't get round to it," she admitted. "He's taken Red out for a ride."

"What?" Ty exclaimed. "He's hardly done anything apart from ride and groom Red all day! There's still the yard to sweep and the hay nets to do and as for all this tack," he swept his hand round the tack-room, "when's that going to get done?"

Amy saw the frustration in his eyes. "Look, don't worry, I'll talk to him when he gets back – I promise."

Amy was sweeping up the loose straw around the muck heap when Ben rode back on to the yard with Red.

He saw her and dismounted. "Working hard?" he said, patting Red.

Amy straightened up, feeling hot and annoyed. She pushed back the hair that stuck to her damp forehead. "Well, someone has to," she said shortly.

Ben looked at her in surprise. "What's up with you?"

"Ben!" burst out Amy, beginning to lose her temper with him. "You're supposed to be working as a stable-hand here. You can't just ride Red all the time and leave all the work to me and Ty!"

"I don't!" Ben protested. "I helped Ty today. I mucked out six stalls and did the lunchtime feeds."

"Big deal!" Amy raised her voice. "What about the other twelve stalls, the tack-cleaning, the grooming – what about working the horses!"

"So are you saying I'm not pulling my weight?" Ben said.

"Yes!"

"OK," he said shortly. "Then I won't ride Red at all in the day. I'll ride him after work."

"Good!" Amy exclaimed. "Perhaps then we can make some progress around here."

"Fine." Ben turned and marched down the yard with Red.

Ty came out of the back barn. "What's all the shouting about?" he said to her.

"Ben," Amy said. She saw Ty open his mouth to speak. "Don't even ask." She sighed. "I guess I'd better go and sort it out or Lou'll be on my back."

She went down the yard telling herself to keep calm. Losing her temper wouldn't do any good. She had to keep reminding herself how Ben had come to be at Heartland in the first place – how they should be grateful for any extra help.

Seeing Ben come out of Red's stall, she went over. "Look, Ben, I didn't mean to go off at you like that. It's just you're going to have to help out more."

"Yeah. Fine," Ben said shortly.

Amy bit back the angry words that jumped to her tongue. "Come on, Ben. It's stupid fighting like this." She thought about the way Red had been in the ring. Maybe that was what was making him so mad. "There are loads of supplements you can use to help calm Red down. Honey's good – and valerian. I'll show you if you like."

"He doesn't need calming down," Ben said, shutting the stall door with a bang. "He just needs to learn discipline."

"Discipline!" Amy exclaimed. "He couldn't even *see* the fence, he was so wound up!"

"He's my horse and I'll decide what methods to use," Ben said angrily.

"Even if they stress him out?" Amy shot back. "Don't be so stubborn, Ben – a herbal supplement might help."

"No way – I'm not giving him any of that rubbish," Ben said.

"Rubbish?" Amy gasped.

"Everyone knows that things like that don't work," Ben said. "Give what you like to the other horses here, but Red's sticking to just his regular feed." He picked up his tack and turned to go, but then hesitated. "Listen, Amy, what you do at Heartland is your prerogative, but just bear in mind that I never *asked* to come here and learn about it all." With that, Ben marched off before Amy could respond.

Right, Amy thought, her temper finally exploding, *that really is the last straw!*

She stormed up to the back barn to find Ty. She had *tried* being patient with Ben. She had tried giving him time. But she was not going to stand around and listen to him rubbish her mom's remedies or show disrespect for their work at Heartland.

"So how did it go?" Ty asked casually. Then he looked at her furious face. "OK – not good."

"You will not *believe* what Ben just said!" Amy exclaimed. The words tumbled out of her as she told Ty about her conversation with Ben.

"He said that?" Ty said.

"Yes!" Amy cried. "This is just so crazy! Why is he here? He doesn't believe in alternative remedies, I hate the way he treats his horse *and* he hardly does any work!" Her eyes flashed. "Well, I've had enough! He's made it quite clear he has no real interest in being here. I'm going to see Lou. We're going to have to do something about him!"

"Like what?" Ty said.

"Get rid of him!" Amy said furiously. "Right away!"

Chapter Six

Amy flung open the back door. Lou was busy updating the accounts on her laptop. She looked round in surprise as Amy burst in.

"I need to talk to you," Amy said.

"What's up?" Lou asked in concern. Just then the phone rang. "Hang on a sec," she said.

Amy sat down impatiently at the table. She wanted to get this sorted out right away. Although the arrangement with Lisa was really convenient, there was no escaping from the fact that Ben just wasn't right for Heartland. He had to go.

"Oh hi, Lisa," Lou said into the phone. "Yes, it's Lou speaking."

Amy turned round in surprise. "Lisa Stillman?" she mouthed at Lou.

Lou nodded at her.

Amy groaned inwardly. *What bad timing!*

"Yes, yes, Ben's settling in just fine," Lou said. Amy started to shake her head frantically, but Lou had turned away and didn't see. "Yes, I'm sure," Amy heard her say. "No, there haven't been any problems. Why, should there be?"

There was a pause. When Lou spoke her voice was serious.

"I understand," she said. "Yes ... yes, I guess it is better that we know."

Amy felt surprised. What was going on?

There was another silence.

"I see," Lou said at last. "Poor Ben."

Amy stared. What *was* Lisa saying?

"Well, like I said," Lou continued. "He seems to have been settling in just fine. But I'll let you know if there are any problems. Yes, of course, we'll keep it to ourselves. You have my word. Thanks for ringing, Lisa. Bye."

"What was that about?" Amy demanded, as Lou replaced the phone in its cradle.

Lou turned, a small frown creasing her forehead. "It's Ben."

"Yeah, I gathered," Amy said impatiently.

Lou sat down slowly at the table. "Look – I'll tell you what she said, if you promise not to repeat it?"

"OK," Amy replied, intrigued. "I promise."

"Lisa was ringing to see how Ben had settled in," Lou explained. "She was worried he might have been a bit difficult. Apparently he's had quite a troubled background and he's had some problems in the past."

"Go on," said Amy, prepared to hear Lou out.

Lou sighed. "Well, his parents divorced when he was ten, and after that he started skipping school and basically getting into trouble. Because his mom wasn't coping very well with the divorce, she felt that maybe it was bad for Ben to be around her. So she sent him to live with Lisa, thinking the change of scene might do him good. Lisa's just told me that it took him a long time to settle in at Fairfield. She thinks that at first he took the move to mean that his mom was abandoning him, just as his dad had done. But then, apparently, he gradually came to realize that he had a natural talent with horses and he began to adjust to and enjoy his new life."

Amy was shocked. "I had no idea."

"Lisa's worried that he sees being moved here as her now abandoning him. That's why she was ringing – to see how he was doing." Lou frowned. "But he's been fine, hasn't he?"

"Well..." Amy wondered what to say. "Actually," she admitted at last, "there have been some problems."

"But the other night you said everything was OK," Lou said quickly.

"No, I didn't," Amy said. "But I didn't get a chance to explain because Scott called. At first I thought it was just because Ben was new and he was settling in. But things have got worse." She told Lou about her argument with Ben and how she had been coming to ask her to fire him.

"I see," Lou said, when she'd finished. She looked at Amy quizzically. "And do you still feel the same?"

Amy hesitated. She felt sorry for Ben but did she feel sorry enough to let him stay? "I don't know," she said slowly.

"Think of what Ben's been through, Amy," Lou said. "We know better than most what it's like to have your father run off and to grow up without having any contact with him. Although logically you know it's not your fault, you can't help blaming yourself. Ben must have felt exactly the same, and now that his aunt's sent him here he's probably feeling pretty hurt and mixed up. I think we just need to be patient and give him some more time."

Amy thought about Ben's earlier outburst. "But why should we?" she demanded. "Worse things have happened to us, and we haven't gone around expecting people to give us special treatment. At least Ben's still got his mom – we haven't!"

"No, we haven't," Lou said quietly. "But what we do have is the knowledge that Mom loved us every minute of her life – despite everything that happened, we've never had any reason to doubt that." She took Amy's hand. "Amy, you grew up here – at Heartland – with both Mom and Grandpa to love and care for you. Ben hasn't had that kind of stability." Lou shook her head. "Think about it, Amy – how would you have felt if Mom hadn't been as strong as she was, and had sent you away after she and Dad separated?"

Amy was silent as Lou's words sank in. It was a thought too horrible to even contemplate.

Lou's voice softened. "Come on, Amy. Don't let's turn our backs on Ben. This must be a difficult time for him and, somehow, I can't help thinking that Heartland might be the best place for him right now." She squeezed Amy's hand. "Can't we at least try and help?"

Slowly, Amy nodded. "OK," she said. "He can stay. I'll … I'll try to be more understanding."

Lou looked relieved. "Thanks, Amy, I really appreciate it. But, you know, I think it might be best if we don't let him know that we're aware of his past," she added. "He might see it as Lisa betraying him. He almost certainly won't want to talk about it and I don't think he'd react well to any special treatment."

"I won't say a word to him," Amy agreed. "And I won't tell anyone – apart from Ty."

"No, Amy. You can't even tell Ty," Lou said hurriedly. "I promised Lisa that what she told me would go no further. I'll explain the situation to Grandpa, but we have to keep it in the family."

Amy was aghast. "I can't keep it secret from Ty! What will he think when I tell him that we're not going to fire Ben? This affects him too. If Ben doesn't pull his weight more and we don't do anything about it, Ty is going to get suspicious."

"Just tell him I insisted that Ben was given a bit more time," Lou said. "Say that we owe it to Lisa because she's financing him being here in the first place. I don't mind if you blame it on me and my accounts. Promise me you won't tell him, Amy."

Amy looked at her reluctantly and sighed. "OK, I promise."

"Listen, Amy," Lou said gently, "things will work out – I'm sure of it. Ben just needs some time." She smiled at her. "We help horses with problems at Heartland – surely we can help him as well?"

Amy walked back on to the yard, deep in thought. Ty was filling a water bucket at the trough. "How did it go?" he said. "What did Lou say?"

"She wants to give Ben a second chance," Amy replied.

"You told her what he said about Heartland and not wanting to be here?" Ty said in surprise.

Amy nodded. "She still said that we should give him more time."

Ty frowned. "How come you aren't mad with her?"

For once, Amy wished that Ty didn't know her so well. "Maybe this time she's right. Perhaps Ben does just need more time to settle in."

She saw Ty look at her in astonishment.

"Anyway, we owe it to Lisa to try and make it work," she said quickly. "And as much as I'm not sure he'll ever fit in, I guess we've got to respect that. Surely a bit of extra help is better than none?"

Ty shrugged but didn't say anything.

"I'll go and talk to him again," Amy said. "Where is he?"

"Bringing Jake and Solo in from the field," Ty said.

Amy smiled weakly and then turned to go up to the turn-out paddocks. She felt awful not telling Ty the entire truth.

She found Ben walking through the gate with the two horses. "Do you want a hand?" Amy said quietly, stepping forward to take Solo's lead-rope.

"Thanks," Ben said.

Amy fidgeted with Solo's lead-rope, not able to look Ben in the eye. This was *so* awkward. "Look..." she started.

"Amy..." Ben began at the same time.

They both stopped. "Go on," Ben said.

"I was just going to say that I'm sorry we argued before," Amy said.

"No, it's me who should be sorry," Ben said ruefully. "I overreacted. You guys have been good to have me here and I just haven't been pulling my weight." He patted Jake. "I'll do a lot more from now on. Sometimes, I just get so focused on Red that I lose track of everything else."

"OK," Amy said, surprised but pleased by his apology. "That would be good."

"I was mad because of how Red had been in the ring," Ben went on. "But I shouldn't have gone off at you like that." The corners of his mouth flickered into a smile. "If I'd been one of the stable-hands at my aunt's place she'd have fired me."

Amy suddenly felt horribly guilty. Ben seemed genuinely sorry about what he'd said earlier. "Oh, we're not going to do that," she said lightly. "Come on."

They began to lead the horses down the yard. "My mom rang me today," Ben said. "She wants to come and watch me and Red at the show." He sounded casual but Amy saw a tightness around his mouth. "I don't see her very often, you know."

"Oh, right. Why ... why not?" Amy said uncomfortably.

Ben shrugged. "My parents divorced when I was ten. Mom didn't deal with it very well and I was shipped out to live with Lisa when I was twelve. I guess Mom thought a break would do me good. It's been pretty permanent, though."

"Has she come to watch Red at shows before?" Amy asked, trying to be positive.

"No," Ben said, and his voice was suddenly quiet. "If she makes it, this will be her first time."

"So, you'll be wanting Red to behave, then," Amy said, trying to sound sympathetic.

"I'd want him to behave whether she was coming or not." Ben put his shoulders back. "I don't care what she thinks."

Amy glanced at him. For a moment he had shown her a much more vulnerable, likeable side – but the barriers were now up again and he had his old determined look back on his face.

As Amy put Solo away, she thought about Ben's words. She didn't believe him when he said that he didn't care what his mother thought. She could tell that he cared deeply. Was that why he had been so hard on Red in the ring earlier? Was it even more important to him now that Red performed well?

Poor Ben, she thought. *Things are pretty complicated for him. Lou's right, it looks like the scars from his past are a long way from being healed.*

For the next few days, when Amy was home from school she noticed that Ben was making more of an effort to help around the yard and he seemed more willing to stay late if necessary. However, it was clear that he was still not interested in learning about Heartland's real work. Although he pulled his weight, he didn't get involved in the healing side of things.

On Saturday, Grandpa collected Flint from Green Briar. When Amy saw the trailer coming back along the drive, she left the stall she was mucking out.

"How is he?" she asked Grandpa as he got out of the truck.

Jack Bartlett raised his eyebrows. "A bit of a handful. He just wouldn't let Claire lead him into the trailer – I had to do it in the end."

"Thanks, Grandpa," Amy said feeling glad that he had been there.

"Are you sure you're going to be able to help Claire with him, Amy?" Jack Bartlett asked, looking concerned. "She's obviously very inexperienced."

"I know, but I do think I can help," Amy said, her grey eyes determined. "I really do."

Her grandpa looked at her for a moment and then smiled

– a smile tinged with sadness. "Sometimes you remind me so much of your mom," he said quietly.

Amy met his eyes. So much of her time was taken up with just carrying on – but the loss and grief was always there and it only took a time like this to bring her feelings flooding to the surface. For a moment the emotion threatened to overwhelm her but just then, Mrs Whitely's car drew up and stopped beside the trailer.

Amy blinked hastily as Claire opened the door and jumped out.

"Wow!" Claire said, looking around at Heartland's barns and paddocks. "It looks just like it did in the magazine."

"Funny, that," Amy said, pushing her feelings back down and forcing her voice to sound light. She smiled at Claire. "I'm glad you like it."

There was a kicking sound from inside the trailer.

"We'd better get this horse out," Jack Bartlett said, beginning to undo the bolts on the ramp and the jockey door.

Glad to have something to do, Amy stepped in through the open door. Claire followed her. Seeing her, Flint flattened his ears and snaked his head forward.

"Here, I'll take him," Amy said, as Claire shrank back. She moved swiftly in beside Flint's neck and untied the lead-rope. Flint shook his head, but she held on. "Easy now," she said, stroking him until he calmed down.

"OK!" she called to her grandpa outside.

Jack Bartlett lowered the ramp and Amy backed Flint out.

Ty and Ben had come to see what was going on. "Nice horse," Ben said appreciatively as Flint snorted and looked round.

"Very," Ty agreed. "Though he looks highly strung."

Claire stepped forward. With a squeal, Flint struck out with his front hoof.

"Be careful, Claire!" her mom gasped.

"He's just unsettled," Amy said, uncomfortably aware of Mrs Whitely's presence. "It's all new to him, that's all." She started to lead Flint around the yard to try and calm him down.

"Can I get you a coffee?" Jack Bartlett offered.

To her relief, Amy saw Mrs Whitely nod. If Flint was feeling wild, then the last thing she wanted was to have Mrs Whitely watching. After all, they were trying to persuade her he was safe.

"So what do you think?" Amy said to Ty.

"Well, he doesn't look naturally aggressive," Ty said.

"You must be joking!" Ben exclaimed. "You saw what he just did."

Ty looked at him impatiently. "Just by looking at his head, you can tell he's not naturally aggressive. He looks intelligent, strong-willed and difficult, but not mean."

Amy smiled at him, delighted that he saw similar traits in Flint's face to those she did.

However, Ben looked less than impressed. "Yeah, and

next you'll be telling me that you're going to check out his star-sign as well!"

Amy tried to explain, hoping to gain his interest. "Ty's right," she said to him. "You *can* tell a horse's personality from its head. The shape of a horse's eyes, ears, muzzle and lips all give you clues as to what it's personality's like."

Claire looked fascinated. "Really? So, what does Flint's head tell you about him?"

Amy looked at the Thoroughbred. "Well, his large eyes and nostrils and slight moose nose suggest that he's intelligent and bold, but his long, flat chin, long mouth and the way his ears are set close together also suggest that he might be strong-willed and difficult. He looks like the sort of horse who needs to respect his rider."

"You can tell all that just from his face?" Claire said in astonishment.

Amy nodded.

"So what am I going do to stop him biting me?" Claire asked.

Amy hesitated. "You'll have to gain his respect. But it might not be easy."

"I don't care," Claire said. "I'm prepared to put in the hours and do whatever it takes to make it work. I just don't want to have to sell him."

"Well, we'll help you all we can," Amy said. "Won't we, Ty?"

"Sure," Ty said. He smiled at Claire. "If you're really

determined to keep him, there's no reason why things shouldn't work out."

"Well, I am," Claire said.

Just then, Mrs Whitely came out of the house. "Are you going to come home with me now, Claire?" she asked.

Claire looked uncertainly at Amy.

"I think it might be best just to let him settle in today," Amy said. "We'll start work on him tomorrow."

"OK," Claire said. "I'll see you tomorrow, then." She glanced at her horse. "Bye, Flint."

The gelding stared into the distance and ignored her.

Claire looked at him for a moment longer and then hurried away.

"So," Amy said, beginning to walk Flint up the yard to the back barn, "do you think Claire will learn to handle him?"

"It's not going to be easy, that's for sure," Ty said seriously.

"You're right there!" Ben said, joining in the conversation. "I'd say it was near enough impossible! It's obvious a girl like that's never going to be able to handle a high-spirited Thoroughbred like Flint – I don't know why you're even bothering."

Ty swung round. He was obviously fed up with Ben's negative attitude. "No," he said. "I guess you wouldn't, would you, Ben?"

"What's that supposed to mean?" Ben demanded, as Amy led Flint into the stall.

"How could *you* possibly understand? You're not remotely interested in how we work around here!" Ty snapped

Amy came to Flint's door. "Ty..." she said, seeing a muscle jump in Ben's jaw.

Ty took no notice of her. He seemed to have worked himself into a real state. "And I don't suppose you've ever known what it's like to really want something, Ben," he said. "To want something so badly that you're prepared to fight for it. You've had it easy all your life. Well, Claire's not as confident as you, but if she wants to fight to keep Flint then we'll help her – Heartland's not just about horses, it's about helping people as well." He shook his head. "Not that I'd ever expect *you* to ever understand *that*." Glaring at Ben, he turned and walked away.

"What's up with him?" Ben exclaimed. "What have I done to deserve that?"

Amy let herself out of the stall, not knowing what to say. Ty hardly ever lost his temper. However, she was sure that Ben's comments about Claire had been the last straw for Ty. The strain of putting in so many hours now that they had a full yard was obviously taking its toll on him. And she understood how frustrating it must be for him to have to tolerate Ben, whose heart just obviously wasn't in it.

"He'll be OK," she said awkwardly. "He's just been working really hard lately and he's tired." She smiled at Ben. Trying to avoid further discussion, she changed the subject. "Look, how about we finish the mucking out and go out for a ride?"

* * *

After she had finished her share of the stalls she went to find Ty. She hadn't seen him since his outburst, deciding that it was best to give him some time to cool off.

He was lunging Moochie in the training ring. When he saw Amy standing at the gate, he brought the big bay hunter to a halt.

"Whoa, there," he said, gathering up the lunge-line and leading the horse over to her.

"Hi," she said.

"Sorry about earlier," he said, rather shamefaced. "I really lost it for a moment back there. Who does Ben think he is? Telling us that we shouldn't be bothering with a horse and rider. That's what Heartland's all about." He shook his head. "You might have gathered that he's really beginning to get to me."

"I noticed," Amy said, with a smile. She cleared her throat, wondering how Ty was going to take the news that she was just about to go on a trail ride with Ben. "I'm going out on the trails with him," she said. "We're going to take Solo and Gypsy." Ty stared at her in astonishment. "They could do with the exercise ... um ... you could come too," she offered quickly.

"No thanks." Ty shook his head. "I don't get it, Amy. Only a few days ago you were as keen as I was to see him fired, and now you'll willingly spend time with him?"

Amy avoided his gaze. "I just think he just needs more

time to get used to this place. I'm trying to make him feel comfortable in the hope that he'll decide to get more involved." She looked up. "Come on, why don't you come? It'll be fun."

"Wild horses wouldn't drag me," Ty said. Then, turning Moochie away from the gate, he walked off.

Amy felt awful. It was as if she had betrayed him. Sure, he'd made light of the situation, but she knew that deep down he must be feeling very confused by the way she was acting.

"See you later, then," she said.

Ty nodded briefly in reply.

Twenty minutes later, Amy and Ben were out on the trails and cantering along a wide, grassy track. Amy glanced across at Ben. He was a very good rider and he controlled the headstrong Gypsy very well. Gypsy was a sixteen-hands, Dutch-bred mare who had been sent to Heartland to have her habit of bucking cured. She was now almost ready to go home. Although she was still a spirited ride, the bucking had stopped.

"Do you want to trot?" Amy called.

Ben nodded and eased the powerful, black mare down into a trot. He patted her neck as she obeyed him.

Amy slowed Solo and brought him into a trot beside Gypsy. "She goes well for you," she said.

"She's a nice horse," Ben said. "What do her owners do with her in the way of competing?"

"Mainly dressage," Amy said. "But I think they hope to do some eventing as well, now she's stopped bucking. She's only five years old."

"How did you stop her bucking?" Ben asked curiously.

"We strapped a dummy on her back and let her buck as much as she wanted until she realized that the dummy wasn't going to come off no matter how much she bucked. Once she realized that her bucking had no effect, she stopped doing it. We changed her diet and used herbs and lavender oil to calm her down, and then we got on her ourselves."

Ben smiled teasingly. "And I guess you analysed her personality as well. That must have helped."

"It did, actually," Amy replied. "If you look at her head you can see that her forehead slopes back from above her eyes to her poll and that she's got a sloping muzzle and narrow nostrils. All those things suggest that she might be stubborn and wilful. We've been working on her to try and encourage her to co-operate with people rather than to resist them."

Ben laughed. "You really believe all that stuff, don't you?"

"Yes," Amy said simply.

"OK, then," Ben challenged her. "So what's Red like?" He grinned. "Go on – analyse his personality."

Amy envisaged the big chestnut horse. "Well, he's got a wide forehead, a long mouth and a flat narrow chin, all of which suggest that he is very intelligent and likely to be a fast learner," she said thoughtfully. "His almond-shaped eyes and fluted nostrils also suggest that he's likely to be trusting and co-operative."

"Go on," Ben said.

"However, the slight dish in his face suggests that he is quite sensitive and needs to be handled carefully. He needs understanding. If you push him too hard he will lose confidence." Amy glanced at Ben. His forehead was furrowed in a slight frown. "Well? What do you think?" she asked. "You know him best. Does my description fit?"

"It's actually not that far off," Ben admitted.

"See!" Amy said, triumphantly.

"Yeah, but you know him quite well now," Ben said quickly. "How do I know that you can tell all that from his head and not just from seeing him about on the yard."

"You don't. You just have to trust me," Amy said. "It's like a lot of our work. Much of it doesn't necessarily seem to make sense but we get the results." She looked at him. "Surely that's what matters."

"Maybe," Ben said. Then he patted Gypsy. "But I prefer to stick to science."

Despite his words, Amy thought that she sensed a slight change in his attitude.

They rode round a bend and the track widened out again. "Come on," she said, deciding not to push him any more for now. "Let's canter!"

Chapter Seven

After lunch, Amy went to check on Flint to see how he was settling in. "I think I'll take him out in the training ring for twenty minutes," she said to Ty.

He nodded. "So have you had any ideas on how to help Claire?"

"Well, first I thought I'd get her to do some T-Touch on him," Amy said. "Then she can start working him from the ground, lunging him at first and then moving on to work him without the lunge-line."

"Good idea," Ty said. "That should help develop the relationship between them. Once they have a good relationship on the ground, then hopefully she should have no problem riding him."

Amy looked at Flint standing at the back of his stall. "He's not exactly what you'd call a friendly horse, is he?"

"Maybe there's something else behind his behavioural

problem," Ty said thoughtfully. "Do you know anything about his history?"

Amy shook her head. Usually she would have asked for all a horse's past details, but she hadn't taken on Flint in the usual way. "I'll ask Claire first thing tomorrow, though," she said. She went into the stall. "Come on then, Flint. Let's do some work."

Like she'd told Ty, she was planning to get Claire to start working Flint from the ground, controlling him with a lunge-line attached to his halter and getting him to walk, trot, canter, change direction, back up and come to the centre when she told him to. The eventual aim was that Claire would be able to work Flint without a lunge-line, using just voice commands. Amy was sure that this sort of work – called liberty work – would help Claire and Flint to develop a bond based on mutual trust and respect.

However, before Claire started work on him Amy wanted to find out whether Flint had ever been lunged before. She snapped the line on to his bridle, picked up the whip and led Flint out of his stall.

Although at Heartland whips were never used to hit a horse, in liberty work the lunge whip was used as a guide for the horse – placed in front of him to slow him down, pointed at his shoulder to keep him out at the sides of the ring or flicked on to the sand to encourage him forward. Marion had always told Amy to think of a lunge whip not as a whip but as an extension of her arm.

Once in the circular training ring, Amy sent Flint out to the end of the lunge-line. It quickly became obvious that he had been through this routine before. On command, he walked, trotted and cantered circles around her.

After ten minutes, Amy decided to start teaching him some new commands. Needing an assistant, she was about to go and call Ty when she caught sight of Ben standing by the muck heap. To her surprise, he seemed to be watching her. In fact, he looked as if he might have been there for a while.

"Hi," she called over to him.

Ben raised his hand in greeting.

Amy made a snap decision. "Do you want to come and help? I could use a hand."

Ben hesitated and then he nodded. "Sure," he called back.

When he reached her, Amy explained what she was going to do. "I need to teach him to change direction on command," she said. "Can you lead him on the outside and then encourage him round when I say 'turn'?"

"Sure," Ben replied.

Amy clicked her tongue and told Flint to walk on. After a few paces, she said, "Turn."

Ben guided Flint round.

They repeated the exercise a few times. "So why are we doing this?" Ben asked.

"It's the first step towards liberty work," Amy said. "You teach the horse the commands on the lunge-line, and when he's learnt the commands you remove the lunge-line to see if he will still obey you when he's free."

"But why?" Ben said.

"Because it helps develop the relationship between horse and rider," Amy explained.

Ben gradually started to move away from Flint's head, until the horse was turning with no guidance apart from Amy's voice.

"We'll make that do for today," Amy said. She was pleased – both with the speed of Flint's learning and with how helpful Ben had been. He might profess not to believe in alternative techniques, but when he dropped his sceptical act he was a very good assistant. He had seemed to sense exactly when Flint had needed his guidance, and when to back away.

"Thanks," Amy said to him. "You were great."

Ben shrugged. "No problem."

As Amy led Flint back to his stall, Ty looked out from Dancer's stall. "How was he?" he asked.

"Great," Amy replied. "I got Ben to help and we started teaching him about turning on command."

"You got *Ben* to help?" Ty echoed.

"Yeah," Amy said, leading Flint into his stall and undoing the bridle. "He was pretty good, actually."

She came out of the stall. Ty was standing in the aisle, his arms crossed, a frown on his face. "I don't get it," he said. "Why are you being so patient with Ben? This isn't like you, Amy."

"Thanks!" Amy said, trying to laugh it off.

But Ty continued to frown. "No, I mean it ... something's going on. All this spending time with Ben – taking his side. Why are you doing it?

"Lou asked me to, you know that," Amy said quickly.

Ty raised his eyebrows. "Yeah, and you always do what Lou says," he said sarcastically. "Come on, Amy. This is me you're talking to."

Amy longed to tell him the truth, but she knew she couldn't. "Well, you know I'm making an effort to listen to Lou a bit more nowadays. And besides, I happen to think that she's right," she said. "Maybe we *should* be giving Ben another chance. Just now he showed that he is capable of learning – he just needs to be approached in the right way." She saw the scepticism in Ty's eyes and her voice rose defensively. "Look, you say it's not like me to be so patient, Ty – well, it's not like *you* to be so judgemental. Why can't you just give Ben a break?"

She saw the hurt flash across Ty's face. Without saying another word he turned and started to walk off.

Amy couldn't bear it. She had to offer some sort of explanation. "OK, OK," she said desperately. "You're right. There *is* something."

Ty swung round.

Amy caught herself. "But ... but I can't tell you what it is."

Ty stared. "You can't tell me?"

Amy saw the disbelief in his eyes. She shook her head. "I've promised Lou," she whispered.

A shutter seemed to fall across Ty's face. "I see," he said coldly.

"I really want to tell you," Amy burst out. "You've got to believe me. But at the same time, I've got to respect Lou's wishes." She looked at him pleadingly. "Please try and understand."

Ty's eyes were icy as he looked at her. "You know, Amy, at the moment I feel like I don't understand you at all." He held her in his gaze. "You've changed," he said curtly, and began walking away. "I've got work to do!"

Amy felt unbelievably terrible. From when Ty had started working full-time at Heartland, her mom had always made a point of telling him everything that was going on; and after she had died, he had been like one of the family – sharing in their grief and fighting with them to keep Heartland going. And now she was keeping something from him and cutting him out of the loop.

She didn't want it to be this way. But she had given Lou her word and she could see that if things could work out for Ben without too many people knowing about his personal life it would be a good thing in the long run. She felt sure that if Ty knew the situation he'd feel the same way.

If only I could tell him, she thought.

That night, when Amy went into the house she went up to

her sister's bedroom. Lou was getting ready for her date with Scott.

"What's up?" she said, seeing Amy hovering at her bedroom door.

"Ty," Amy said, sighing. "Lou, I feel I've just *got* to tell him about Ben."

"I understand, Amy – I really do," Lou said gently. "But please, let's give Ben a bit more time. Ty'll come round as Ben finds his place with us." She stepped forward, her eyes sympathetic. "I'm really sorry to have to put you in this situation but I want to honour my word to Lisa. Grandpa agrees with me – it's the decent thing to do."

Amy didn't say anything. She could see Lou's point of view. She knew that if she were Ben and she found out that they were all aware of her past, she'd resent them discussing her problems. If she were in his position, she'd want a fresh start and the chance to leave the past behind.

"I'm sorry," Lou went on. "I *know* it's hard for you and that I'm putting you in an awkward position, but you'll be doing me a huge favour by trusting me on this one."

"It's ... fine," Amy sighed, wishing it could be different.

Lou smiled. "Thanks, Amy. And listen, I'm here for you if you want to talk. You know that, don't you?"

Amy nodded. "What time's Scott coming round?" she asked.

"Any minute now," Lou said, glancing at her watch. "I'd better get a move on or I'll be late."

Suddenly, there was the sound of a car arriving outside. Amy looked out of the window. "Scott's here!" she said, smiling at her sister.

Lou followed Amy down the stairs as she raced to open the door.

"Hi, Amy," Scott said, as he came into the kitchen. He caught sight of Lou. "Hey," he said, "you look great!"

"Thanks," Lou said, blushing. "So do you." Going even redder, she started looking round quickly. "I'll ... I'll just get my coat."

"It's in the hall," Amy said, secretly enjoying the way the usually very-together Lou seemed to be falling to pieces now that Scott was here. It was good to see her sister's more vulnerable side sometimes.

Lou reappeared from the hall with her coat and Scott opened the door.

"Have a great time, kids," Amy teased.

"We intend to," Scott said, smiling at Lou.

Amy woke up in the early hours of Sunday morning. She heard the sound of the door shutting and a car driving off. Glancing at the luminous hands on her bedside clock, she saw that it was 2 a.m. She smiled. Things must have gone well!

There was no sign of Lou when Amy got up. It was Ty and Ben's day off, but as usual Ty turned up to help. He was quiet as they gave out the feeds.

"I'll get on with the stalls in the back barn," he said to her once the horses had been fed and watered. Hardly even waiting for her answer, he hurried off.

Amy sighed. She hated keeping a secret from him, and things were worse now that he knew she was hiding something. But she didn't know what to say to patch up things between them.

After a bit, Amy saw Lou come out of the house. She hurried over. "So how did it go?" she asked eagerly.

Despite still looking half asleep, Lou smiled. "It was wonderful! We just had so much to talk about."

"So are you going out again?" Amy said.

"Maybe," Lou said.

"When?" Amy demanded.

Lou smiled. "Tonight."

"Oh, Lou! That's great!" Amy said, hugging her in delight. "Wait till I tell Matt and Soraya!"

Claire arrived later in the morning. "OK, come on into the stall," Amy said, holding Flint by the halter. Claire walked in nervously. Flint put his ears back. "No!" Amy told him sharply. "It's OK, Claire. Just come up to him and pat him," she said kindly.

She made Flint stand still as Claire patted him.

"First, you're going to learn how to do some T-Touch," Amy said. She showed Claire how to use the pads of her fingers to push Flint's skin lightly over his muscles in small circles.

"After you've finished one complete circle, slide your fingers to a new part of his neck and do another," Amy said. "And go slowly. The slower you go the more he will relax."

Amy watched Flint's eyes carefully. He didn't look like he was particularly enjoying it, but neither was he objecting to Claire touching him. After a minute or two, he seemed to relax slightly.

"Go all along his neck, the top of his back and hindquarters," Amy said.

After ten minutes, she let go of Flint's halter. He stood quietly while Claire worked.

"I like doing this," Claire said, looking up.

"We use it on all the horses here," Amy said. "It's particularly good for those who are tense or over-sensitive, or if you need to improve your relationship with a horse."

After a bit, they took Flint up to the ring. Amy lunged him first. He was excited to start with but after he had cantered several circles and thrown in a couple of high-spirited bucks, he began to calm down and to listen to Amy's commands.

"OK, you can take over now, Claire," Amy said, bringing him to a halt.

"He looks a bit lively," Claire said uneasily.

"He'll be fine," Amy replied. "Trust me."

Claire reluctantly came into the ring. Amy smiled at her reassuringly and handed her the lunge-rope before moving to the gate.

"Walk on," Claire said hesitantly.

Flint didn't move.

"Walk on." Claire's voice shook as she moved the whip towards him.

Flint stamped his hoof into the sand and put his ears back threateningly. Claire quickly withdrew the whip. "He's not moving," she said looking helplessly at Amy.

"Sound like you mean it," Amy said, feeling slightly exasperated.

Claire tried again, but this time Flint moved towards her – his ears flat. Claire gasped and jumped back. "Amy!" Her foot caught in the folds of the lunge-rope that was carelessly hanging from her hand. With a cry she stumbled to the ground.

Flint reared up in surprise.

"No!" Claire cried, covering her face with her hands.

Amy was already scrambling over the gate. She reached Flint just as he came to the ground. "Easy now!" she said, grabbing hold of his bridle.

Snorting loudly, the Thoroughbred stared at Claire.

"Are you OK?" Amy demanded.

Claire nodded. "I thought he was going to attack me!" she said, getting to her feet.

"It's OK. You just startled him," Amy said. "He wasn't trying to attack you when he reared." She looked at Flint's tense eyes. This was getting them nowhere. "Right, how about you watch for a bit more?" she said to Claire, who nodded gratefully.

She worked Flint for twenty minutes and then looked towards the gate. She knew Claire needed to work with Flint, but he was being so good for her. It would be really frustrating if Claire took over and he played up, and they had to finish the training session on a bad note.

She asked the grey gelding to halt. "I think I'll bring him in now," she called to Claire.

"OK," Claire said, looking relieved that she wasn't going to have to work him again.

Amy led Flint over to the gate. "So, do you know anything about Flint's past?" she asked, remembering her conversation with Ty the other day.

"Um, a bit," Claire replied. "I know he was bred by a woman who kept him until he was five before selling him on. He's six now and I think he's had two other owners besides me in the last year."

"So, it sounds like he hasn't had a very secure time," Amy said. "Maybe the constant changing of owners and barns could be contributing to Flint's behavioural problems. With three different owners in a year, it's no wonder he's feeling unsettled."

"I hadn't thought about it like that," Claire said. "But I guess you're right. It can't have been very easy for him." She smiled rather sadly. "I know how he feels."

Amy looked at her curiously. "What do you mean?"

"Well, since Mom and Dad separated, Mom's always getting new jobs and we keep moving," Claire explained. "I constantly have to start at different schools and make friends over again. Like Flint, I guess. Since the divorce I haven't really had anywhere I could call home."

"It can't be easy for you, either," Amy said.

Claire shrugged. "I manage." Her voice lifted. "Mom seems to really like it round here, though – maybe she won't want to move again. And we're nearer to where my dad lives so I can visit him more regularly. He's away at the moment but I can't wait for him to come back and see Flint again."

"Well, now we know what's been happening to Flint, we can use some essential oils or flower remedies to help calm him down," Amy said. "As he gets calmer he'll hopefully become more receptive to forming a new relationship with you. The T-Touch will help too – and so will working him from the ground."

"I hope he improves around me soon," Claire said hopefully.

Amy smiled reassuringly at her. "I'm sure he will."

Ben arrived at lunchtime. "I'll give you a hand with the rest of the work when I've finished riding Red," he said when Amy went to say hi.

"But it's your day off," Amy said in surprise.

He shrugged. "I haven't got anything else to do."

"Well then, thanks," Amy said, smiling at him, pleased that he was making a bit more of an effort.

"Mom rang again last night," Ben told her as they walked to the tack-room together. "I thought she might be ringing to cancel – like she has before – but she said she's definitely going to come." He picked up his grooming kit. "I'd better get moving – Red and I've got some practice to do."

Amy sat down to clean some tack. After a while, Ben led Red up to the training ring. She was just putting a saddle back on its rack when Ty came marching into the tack-room.

"That's it!" he exclaimed, his eyes dark and angry. "I've had enough. That guy's the limit!"

Amy didn't think she had ever seen Ty look so furious. "What is it?" she said, alarmed.

"Just come and see what he's doing to Red!" Ty exclaimed. He stormed out of the tack-room.

Amy ran after him. "Ty! Wait!" But Ty didn't stop.

She hurried up to the training ring to find Ben cantering a very wound-up-looking Red in small circles in front of a jump.

"What does he think he's doing?" Ty demanded, as Red fought for his head, his mouth foaming with saliva. "Could he get that horse any more stressed? I can't stand by and watch this."

Amy took a deep breath and tried to rationalize the situation. She *hated* her new role as diplomat! "He's just trying to stop Red rushing his fences," she said quickly. "Listen – this show he's going to in a few weeks is really important to him." Like Ty, she hated seeing Ben ride Red in such a way and she wished he would stop, but she was trying hard to understand him now that she knew why he was so keen for Red to do well in the show.

Ty turned on her. "So, you approve of what he's doing?" he said incredulously.

"Of course I don't," Amy said. "But what can we do – Red's Ben's horse!"

"And he's riding him on Heartland property," Ty said. His mouth hardened. "Well, if you won't say anything, Amy, I will."

"Wait, Ty!" Amy pleaded.

But it was too late. Ty was already striding to the fence. "What do you think you're doing, Ben?" he exclaimed.

Ben pulled Red to a halt. "What?" he said in surprise.

"Riding Red like that – look at him." Ty pointed to the sweat foaming on Red's neck. "Have you gone crazy?"

Ben's eyes grew colder. "Can't you see he's rushing at the jumps?"

"Oh, right, and you think stressing him out like that is going to stop it?" Ty demanded.

"Like you know anything about it!" Ben snapped.

"I know that if you get a horse – any horse – into a state like that it won't be able to even think, let alone learn," Ty snapped back. "It's the most stupid thing I've ever seen."

"Well, thanks for your opinion," Ben said, digging his heels into Red's sides so that the horse broke into a canter again. "But I don't need your help."

Amy could see the situation getting out of hand. "Ty, look ... just leave it," she said, rushing over.

He swung round. "Leave it? *Leave it!*" For a moment,

Amy thought he was going to grab her shoulders and shake her, but then he seemed to stop himself. "This isn't like you, Amy," he said, his voice quiet and intense. "You've always been the first to make a stand when you see a horse being mistreated."

"Ben's not mistreating Red … at least, he's not actually being cruel," Amy argued desperately.

Ty looked at the ring where Red was being forced to canter in tiny circles, his head bent, his neck foaming with sweat. "So you think that *that*'s not mistreating a horse?" he said, turning so that his eyes bored into hers.

Amy didn't say anything – she couldn't. She knew he was right. This whole stupid situation was breaking her heart.

Ty's eyes held hers for a moment and then, shaking his head in angry disbelief, he pushed past her and walked away.

Chapter Eight

For the rest of that day, Amy felt that Ty was avoiding her. Instead of hanging around to talk to like he usually did, he left straight after the horses had been fed.

"What's been up with him today?" Ben asked, joining her as she watched Ty's car bump away down the drive.

Amy shrugged. There was no way she was getting into this conversation with him. "Oh ... I don't know. I guess he's just in a bad mood."

"If you ask me, he's in a permanently bad mood," Ben said. "Doesn't that guy *ever* lighten up?"

"You don't know him," Amy said defensively. "He's OK."

"Yeah, if you're a three-legged psycho horse," Ben said.

Amy glared at him and walked away.

"Hey, Amy! I'm sorry," Ben said, going after her.

She stopped.

"Look, don't get me wrong," Ben sighed. "I know you and Ty get along really well and that he's great with the horses you get here, but I sure wish he'd stop trying to tell me how to train my horse."

"He only said those things because he cares," Amy said.

"Are you saying I don't?" Ben demanded

"I sometimes wonder..." Amy began.

"Amy – Red is *the* most important thing in my life," Ben interrupted her. "I would never do anything to harm or hurt him in any way."

"What about this *afternoon*?"

"You and Ty might not agree with my methods," Ben went on. "But they're *my* methods and I'm using them with *my* horse and if either of you don't like that, then that's your problem – not mine. I'm not the only person who uses these kind of techniques, you know."

Amy took a deep breath. Part of her wanted to yell at him to stop being so stubborn, to listen to Ty – to listen to her. But she knew it wouldn't do any good. She couldn't force him to change his training methods, trying to do so would only turn him against her – as well as against Ty. All she could do was be patient, give him time and try to win him over.

The atmosphere on the yard did not improve over the next few days. Ty avoided Ben as much as possible and was distinctly cool with Amy when she was around on the yard. To take her mind of it, Amy threw herself into working Flint.

Claire came to Heartland every night after school. She was getting increasingly confident using the T-Touch circles and massaging him with diluted essential oils, a remedy that Amy hoped would help settle him down. In the stall, at least, Flint seemed to be accepting Claire more and more. But as soon as he was out in the training ring, everything changed.

Faced with trying to control Flint in an open space, Claire seemed to lose all confidence and always ended up giving the lunge-line to Amy and going to watch from the gate.

Amy told herself that it didn't matter. They were just taking things slowly and it was better that Flint was at least learning the voice exercises with her. She also had to admit that she loved working Flint. His intelligence meant that although he was a challenge he was also a very quick learner, and she quickly sensed a bond growing between them.

On Friday afternoon when she went up to his stall after school, he was looking out over his stall door. When he saw her, he whinnied softly.

Amy was delighted. It was one of the first signs of affection that Flint had shown. She hurried forward, digging a packet of mints out from her pocket. "Hi, boy."

He pushed his dark-grey muzzle softly against her arm as she took a mint from the packet.

Just then, Ty came out of Dancer's stall.

"He's getting friendlier," he said, looking at Flint nuzzling Amy.

She nodded. "Did you hear him whinny?"

"Yeah."

Amy glanced up. Ty was watching her. "What?" she said, seeing concern in his eyes.

"He's supposed to be forming a bond with Claire, Amy, not with you."

"I know," Amy said quickly.

"So why are you working him each day?" Ty said.

"Well, Claire doesn't want to," she said defensively. "And anyway I'm not working him in the stall, Claire's doing all the T-Touch now." She saw that Ty's eyes were still looking concerned. "Claire just needs more time to become more confident!"

"She'll never gain confidence while you do everything for her," Ty said.

"But if she starts doing the ground exercises now, Flint could get worse," Amy protested. "I'm just thinking about him!"

"You're supposed to be thinking about Claire too," Ty said. "Or have you forgotten that?"

Amy felt hot blood sting her cheeks. Deep down, she knew he was right, but she didn't want him to be. She liked working Flint and she really was concerned about how his behaviour might change if she made Claire work him instead. "I'm the one that's supposed to be treating him!" she said. "And I'll make the decisions!"

Ty stared at her. "*You*'ll make the decisions?" He stared at her. "I thought we treated the horses *together*, Amy."

Amy swallowed, her cheeks going redder as she realized what she had just said. "I ... I didn't mean it..." She felt horribly uncomfortable. She had never spoken to Ty in such a way before. Since her mom had died they had both decided on the treatment of the horses – as equals.

Just then, Claire appeared at the top of the aisle. "Hi!" she called out, oblivious to the tension in the air. She hurried towards them. "How are you, Ty?"

"Fine," he replied, stepping back from Amy. He smiled briefly at Claire. Amy had noticed that he always seemed to make a special effort to be friendly towards her.

"I've got a favour to ask," Claire said, looking at them both.

"Ask away," Ty said.

"Well, when we bought Flint here, I was in such a rush to get away from Green Briar that I left three of his rugs there." Claire looked awkward. "I don't want to go there on my own in case Ashley's there. I was hoping that..."

"That one of us would come with you?" Ty finished for her.

Claire nodded. "Would you?" she said hopefully.

"Sure," Ty said with a shrug. "We can go in my car."

"Yeah, I'll come as well," Amy said. She smiled at Claire, trying to forget the argument with Ty. "We'll protect you from Ashley."

They got into Ty's car. Still oblivious to the tension crackling between him and Amy, Claire chattered away. Now she had got over being shy she was good fun to be with.

When they reached Green Briar, there was no sign of Ashley or Val Grant. "I'll go with Claire to get the rugs," Amy said to Ty. "It'll only take us a few minutes."

Ty nodded. "I'll wait here."

Amy and Claire found Flint's rugs. "At least we haven't seen the Grants," Claire said as they hurried back across the yard.

"Don't speak too soon," Amy said. As they turned the corner towards the car, she had seen Ashley leaning against it, talking to Ty.

Claire stopped dead. "Oh no."

"Come on," Amy urged her. "Just stand up to her."

Ashley's back was turned to them. As they got nearer, they saw her flick her hair back and laugh and then lean closer to Ty.

Amy felt a surge of anger. She gritted her teeth and marched towards them.

"We could really use someone with your talents at Green Briar, Ty," she heard Ashley say. On the word *talents*, Ashley's voice dropped huskily. "You know, my mom is desperate to have you work here."

"Ty's already got a job, Ashley!" Amy said.

Ashley turned. "Hi there, Amy," she said coolly. "Ty and I were just..." She glanced back at Ty. "Chatting."

"Yeah, I heard!" Amy said angrily. "Well, Ty's not leaving Heartland. Are you, Ty?"

Ty gave a small shake of his head but glared at Amy. Amy

cursed herself. She knew she shouldn't have spoken for him like that, but she was worried and couldn't help herself. Things had been so difficult at Heartland lately, she couldn't help thinking that Ty might actually be tempted by the Grants' offer. If he was, she guessed she couldn't blame him.

"Pity," Ashley went on, looking at Ty through her long eyelashes. "We could have *such* fun. Still," she said, "it's not too late to change your mind. The position's still vacant. In fact, Mom's getting so desperate, you could probably name your price."

Amy threw the rugs on to the back seat of the car. "Come on! Let's go!" She felt so mad with Ashley that she could have almost hit her. How dare Ashley try and talk Ty into going to Green Briar right in front of her! Seeing Ashley smile at Ty again, she almost exploded. "I said let's go!" she snapped, flinging herself into the front seat. She realized she was behaving badly but this whole scene was making her feel ill. *Oh, if only things were normal between Ty and me*, she thought.

"See you," Ty said to Ashley.

Amy slammed the door.

Claire hastily got into the back seat. "Too scared to come without reinforcements?" Ashley said to her, a sneer in her voice. "How pathetic."

Claire looked away.

"Bye, Ty," Ashley said, as Ty started the engine. "And remember what I said."

* * *

Amy was so wound up that she didn't say a word all the way back to Heartland. Once they arrived, she went straight to the feed-room and tried to work off her anger by making up the evening hay nets.

Claire came to find her. "Flint's ready," she said.

"OK," Amy said. She was hot from shaking up the hay and stuffing it furiously into the nets, but she felt slightly calmer.

"Ashley really got to you, didn't she?" Claire said tentatively as they walked down to the tack-room together to get Flint's bridle and the lunging equipment. "Was it the way she was coming on to Ty?"

"Don't even mention Ashley to me," Amy muttered angrily.

"Oh ... OK," Claire said. There was a pause. "So ... what are you going to do with Flint tonight?"

Amy thought about Ty's words. Claire did need to start working Flint.

"Well, I'll work him on voltes – they're small circles," Amy said. "And then I think you should have a go. See what he does."

Claire looked panic-stricken. "Can't we wait a bit longer? I mean, he's being so good for you."

"Yeah, but he needs to be good for you," Amy said. "He's been loads better with you in the stall. If you're firm with him, I think you'll find he'll be good outside as well."

Claire didn't look convinced.

Amy worked Flint for five minutes and then decided that

it was time for Claire to have a go. She halted Flint and called to Claire who was standing at the gate. "Come into the middle."

"Are you sure?" Claire said nervously.

Amy nodded. "You'll be fine."

Claire walked cautiously into the centre of the ring.

"Just stand beside me as I lunge him," Amy said. She sent Flint forward at a trot again and after three circles gave Claire the lunge-rein. "Right, you take over."

"No," Claire said quickly, trying to hand back the line.

"Go on," Amy said, refusing to take it. "It's OK."

But sensing Amy's lack of concentration, Flint slowed down and looked towards the middle. "Tell him to trot on," Amy said quickly to Claire.

"Trot on!" Claire said nervously.

Flint slowed to a walk.

"Go on – make him do it," Amy said more firmly.

But Claire shook her head and gave the lunge-line back to Amy. "You do it – he'll do it for you."

With a sigh, Amy took back the line.

"Amy!" She looked towards the gate and saw Ty there. She wondered how long he had been watching.

"What?" she called.

"I need to speak to you a minute."

Amy brought Flint to a halt. "Can't it wait?"

"No," Ty said.

Amy called Flint to her. The grey horse walked over

obediently. Amy turned him to bring him in, wondering what it was that Ty needed to talk about so urgently.

"Claire will hold him for you, won't you, Claire?" Ty said.

Claire looked startled. "Well ... er..."

"We won't be long," Ty said smiling at her. "Just walk him round. Do some T-touch with him."

"OK," Claire agreed.

Amy walked over to the gate. "Yeah?"

"Let's not talk here," Ty said. "Come down on the yard."

Amy followed him away from the gate. "So, what's so important?" she demanded.

"Claire's relationship with Flint," Ty said. "You have to let her work him on her own."

Amy stared at him. "What exactly do you think I was trying to do? I virtually forced her to take the lunge-rope from me."

"But then you took it back." Ty shook his head. "I know you're only trying to help, Amy. But don't you see? While you're there, Claire's never going to stand a chance. Flint will turn to you for direction and Claire is so in awe of you that she won't even try."

"So you expect me just to leave her to it?" Amy said. "Yeah, good one, Ty! You know what happened last time I tried that."

"But she's been doing the T-Touch on him since then," Ty said. "Their relationship has improved."

"Not enough!" Amy said.

"Give her a chance, Amy," Ty insisted.

Amy shook her head. "I have to think of Flint. It'll confuse him. The horse has to come first."

Ty looked at her. "But not if it's Ben and Red?"

Amy was stung. "That's not fair!"

"Isn't it?" Ty said.

"No, it's not!" she cried angrily. "I don't like the way Ben treats Red any more than you do, but there's nothing we can do about it. Look, if you're so keen to understand Claire, couldn't you be a bit more understanding about Ben?"

Ty laughed scornfully. "What's there to understand? He's a spoilt rich kid who cares more about winning than he does about his horse."

"That is *not* true!" Amy said. "Ben does care – he cares a lot."

"Well, he's sure got a strange way of showing it!" Ty snapped. He shook his head. "I just don't get the way you defend him the whole time. Like I said the other day, you've changed, Amy. I don't know why, but you have, and it's affecting things here. I came here to work for your mom and follow her ideals, but right now Heartland's just not the same." The phone started to ring. "I'll get it," he said, and he marched away.

Feeling angry, Amy hurried back to the ring. Right now, she just felt like she was under too much pressure, and it was all beginning to get to her. As she turned the corner, she stopped dead. Claire was standing in the middle of the ring and was sending Flint to the outside.

"Away!" Amy heard her say. Flint hesitated and Claire flicked the ground with the whip. "Go on! Away!"

Flint walked to the outside.

Amy took a step back. She didn't want Claire to see her in case it put her off. Was she actually going to try to lunge him?

She saw Claire tap the lunge whip on the ground. "And trot!"

Flint looked at her. "Trot on!" Claire said, using the whip on the ground again.

To Amy's surprise, Flint began to trot. She saw a look of astonishment cross Claire's face. "And walk!" she told him, positioning the whip just in at the point of his shoulder. as Amy normally did. Flint slowed to a walk.

"Good boy!" Claire praised. "And turn!"

Claire almost tripped over the lunge-line as Flint did as she said. "And trot on!" she called. An amazed smile lit up her face as Flint broke into a trot again.

Amy felt a surge of delight, but she stopped herself from running up to the gate. She didn't want to disturb Claire when she was doing so well.

After a few more minutes, Claire brought Flint to a halt again and then called him to the middle. He walked over.

"Good boy!" she cried, stepping forward to pat him.

Flint threw his head in the air and for a moment Amy's heart stopped as she thought Claire was about to shrink back – but, emboldened by her lunging success, Claire didn't.

"No!" Amy heard her say firmly. Taking up the slack on the rope, Claire stepped closer and patted the grey's neck again.

This time, Flint accepted it. He snorted and then, bringing his head round, he looked at her. For the first time, Amy could see a glimmer of respect in his eyes.

Claire rubbed his forehead and smiled.

A wave of relief and delight overwhelmed Amy. The war wasn't over yet for Claire and Flint, but she knew the first battle had been won. She longed to tell Ty. Suddenly, all the arguments of the past ten days faded into the past; nothing mattered but being able to tell him and have him share her delight.

It's so stupid arguing with him, she thought, running down the yard to look for him. *Where would I be without Ty? He's the only one who really understands!*

She looked in the feed- and tack-rooms and then remembered the phone ringing. She ran towards the open kitchen door. As she got near she heard his voice – he was still on the phone. She slowed down, not wanting to disturb him.

"Yeah, the salary is extremely generous," she heard him saying. "And two days off a week sounds great."

Salary? Amy stopped. *Days off?*

There was a pause.

"Yeah, of course I'll let you know, Mrs Grant," she heard Ty say.

Mrs Grant! Amy froze. Val Grant was talking to Ty about

salaries and days off. And he was saying he'd let her know. Surely he couldn't really be considering taking the job at Green Briar?

She backed away from the house, then turned and ran up the yard and into the feed-room. She sat down on a bale of hay, her stomach churning. Ty couldn't leave. How could she run Heartland without him? She buried her head in her hands and tried to fight back the tears.

A few minutes later, she heard footsteps coming up to the barn. Wiping the arm of her sweatshirt across her face, she jumped to her feet.

Ty entered. He stopped when he saw her. "What are you doing in here?" He frowned. "What's up?"

"Nothing," she said quickly.

"Have you been crying?" he said, stepping closer.

"No." Amy looked down as she felt the tears rise in her throat again.

"Amy?" Ty took hold of her arm. "What's wrong?"

"Nothing's wrong!" Amy cried, hurt and betrayal flooding through her, as she looked at his concerned, familiar face. How could he look like that when he was planning on leaving? She knew things hadn't been easy for him since Ben had arrived, but she didn't think things had become as drastic as this. Although she hadn't been very communicative with Ty of late, she would still have expected him to tell her if things felt *so* seriously wrong for him. Suddenly something snapped inside her.

She wrenched her arm away. "Get off me!" she screamed at him. "I hate you! Leave me alone!"

Ty's face paled, as if he had been hit. He stepped backwards and then swung round again, out of the barn.

Amy collapsed on to the hay bale again, and this time completely gave way to her tears.

Chapter Nine

Ten minutes went by before Amy had enough control of herself to go up to the training ring. She splashed some water on her face from Flint's water bucket and then went up to the ring. She had a responsibility – Mrs Whitely trusted her with Claire and Flint's well-being. Amy took several deep breaths. What would Claire be doing?

She was lunging Flint again. He was cantering round her. Seeing Amy she brought him to a halt. "Look!" she said in delight. "He's letting me lunge him!"

"That's great," Amy said, going into the school.

Claire frowned. "Are you OK? You look … odd."

Amy managed a faint smile. "I'm OK, thanks."

"What did Ty want?"

"Oh, just to talk about one of the horses," Amy lied. She patted Flint. "It really is great that you've been working him on your own."

"I know!" Claire said, caught up in her own delight. "I walked him round for a bit and then did some T-Touch. He was being good so I thought I'd just try lunging him – and he was fine." She grinned. "I can't wait to tell Mom!"

When Claire told Ty about her success with Flint, he congratulated her warmly. "I knew you could do it!" he said.

"Thanks," Claire said, smiling at him. "I know I'm going to have to work hard each day to try and build a really good relationship with him, but at least it's a start."

"It certainly is," Ty said.

After Claire had gone, Ty hardly said a single word to Amy until he left that evening. "I'm taking my day off tomorrow," he said curtly, as he got his coat from the tack-room. "So, I'll see you Sunday."

Amy nodded. "Bye."

She watched Ty walk away, thoughts tumbling through her mind in a confused mess. Part of her wanted to run after him, to beg him not to leave Heartland, to tell him that she couldn't run the place without him. But there was another part of her that felt desperately hurt, and utterly furious, that he could consider betraying her by going to Green Briar.

She swallowed. What was she going to do?

The next morning, Claire arrived at nine o'clock. Amy had never seen her at Heartland so early before. "I can't wait to try lunging him again," she said. "Mom's not going to collect me till this afternoon. I thought maybe I could lunge him twice?"

"Sure – as long as you keep both sessions short," Amy said.

"I could do some T-Touch on him in between," Claire said. "And groom him."

Claire's first lunging session with Flint went well and the second went even better. Amy watched from the gate. "You're doing great!" she said encouragingly.

Just then, Ben joined her. "She has got better, hasn't she?" he said.

Amy nodded. "It's all down to confidence," she said, as Claire made Flint turn and canter in the opposite direction. "Now she knows she can make Flint do what she wants, her confidence is just growing and growing. Hey Claire!" she called. "How about trying him without the lunge-line."

Claire brought Flint to a halt. "What? Really?"

"Yeah," Amy said. "Just use the whip as you've been doing with the line on," Amy said. "Let's see what he does."

Claire led Flint over to the gate, unsnapped the lunge-line and handed it to Amy. "Here goes."

She led Flint back to the centre and then let go of his bridle. "Away," she told him. Flint obediently walked away and then suddenly he seemed to realize that the lunge-line was missing. He stopped.

"Use the whip!" Amy said quickly.

Claire tapped the whip on the floor. "Walk on."

Flint hesitated. Amy held her breath but then, to her relief, the grey horse moved on.

"And trot!" Claire said quickly, tapping the whip on the floor again.

With no line attaching him to her, Flint broke into a trot. He trotted fluently around the circle.

"And turn!" Claire called.

Spinning quickly on his haunches, Flint changed direction.

"That's amazing!" Ben said to Amy.

"Well done!" Amy shouted.

After a few more circuits, Claire brought Flint to a halt and called him to her. "I'll make that do!" she said, patting him in delight. "I'll do some more tomorrow. But wasn't he brilliant?"

"You both were!" Amy said, opening the gate as Claire led Flint over.

"I never believed that I'd be able to do it," Claire said, looking totally astonished. Her eyes shone. "Did you see the way he changed the rein? He was so quick!"

Amy nodded. She had and, more importantly, she had seen the respect and trust in Flint's eyes as he had willingly obeyed Claire's commands.

"He's like a different horse," Ben said to her as they followed Claire and Flint down the yard. "I mean, I saw him myself – only a week ago he wouldn't let her near him."

"And now he's doing what she wants," Amy agreed. "Not

because he's forced to but because he chooses to. It's a partnership, and the stronger the bond between them gets the harder he will try for her." She looked at him. "Having a horse who tries his heart out for you – isn't that what every top competitor wants?"

Hoping her words would sink in, she walked away. The only way things were going to work out at Heartland was if she could get Ben to start working the way she and Ty did. If they had to let Ben go, they would be under the same strain they had been a few weeks ago – and with her at school it was just too much for Ty to cope with. Of course, that was if Ty was planning on sticking around. Amy felt sick. She just had to make things work for *everyone*.

Before Claire left that afternoon, she asked Amy whether she could let her mom see Flint work the next day.

"Sure," Amy said.

"I think she'll be really impressed," Claire said happily. "Right, see you tomorrow, then!"

"Yeah, see you," Amy replied.

She thought about the next day. How would Ty behave? How was she going to act around him? Should she tell him that she had overheard his phone conversation with Val Grant? But how awkward would that be? She couldn't tell him that she had listened to his private conversation – and if she did, and he said that he was leaving... What would she do *then*?

* * *

Amy was mucking out a stall when Claire and her mom arrived on Sunday morning.

"Hello, Amy," Mrs Whitely said. "Claire said it was OK if I came to watch today."

Amy nodded. "Sure."

"I'll go and groom Flint, shall I, and get him out?" Claire said eagerly

"Yes, but do some T-Touch on him first," Amy said.

"OK," Claire said. She turned to her mom. "Come on, Mom – come and see what T-Touch is." Her eyes lit up. "You could even do some!"

Amy looked at Claire in surprise. She had never seen her look so happy and enthusiastic. The success of the day before really seemed to have changed her. *I just hope that Flint's as good with her today*, Amy thought. *It will be awful if he plays up with Mrs Whitely here.*

Five minutes later, Ben arrived. It was his day off. He came to find her. "I'm going to take Red out for a ride," he said. "Do you want to come?"

"Thanks, but I'd better not – Mrs Whitely is here to see Claire work Flint." Amy said. She put her pitchfork down. "I hope he's good."

Ben nodded. "I'm sure he will be. See you later, then."

Amy finished the stall and decided to go and see how Claire was getting on. As she walked up the yard, she saw Ben setting off on Red.

"Have a good ride," she called.

Claire was working T-Touch circles on Flint's forehead. Flint's neck was low and relaxed and his eyes half closed. Amy felt relieved.

Mrs Whitely smiled when she saw Amy. "Claire's been explaining this T-Touch to me – it's fascinating."

Claire looked round. "Shall I take him into the ring now, Amy?"

Amy nodded. "Start off on the lunge-rope and then when he's settled you can let him off."

Claire set off to the tack-room.

Mrs Whitely watched her go. "I can't believe the change in Claire," she said to Amy. "She's been so happy in the last few days. She's hardly stopped talking for a moment!"

Amy nodded. "I think it's really helped her confidence to be able to get Flint to do what she wants."

"So she really is OK to handle him on her own?" Mrs Whitely asked. "When she said I could come and watch her today, I have to admit I had my doubts – this improvement seems to have occurred very quickly."

"We've been treating him with some violet-leaf oil to help calm him down, and the T-Touch Claire's been doing each day with him has helped develop a bond between them," Amy explained. "But the real breakthrough came when Claire worked him on her own yesterday." She saw Mrs Whitely look curious. "I think she suddenly realized that if she was firm, he would do what she wanted and so she stopped feeling so scared of him," Amy went on. "Flint has started to respect her, and now, hopefully, their relationship can develop into a real partnership."

"You know an impressive amount for a fifteen-year-old," Mrs Whitely said.

"My mom taught me," Amy said. "Now she's not here, Ty and I work together with the horses."

As the words left her mouth, she realized what she was saying. Her breath caught in her throat. It was so natural to talk about Ty and her working the horses together – but for how much longer? He had hardly spoken a word to her since that morning, and whenever she had caught sight of him going about the yard his face had been set and his eyes hard.

Just then, Claire came back. "OK," she said, snapping the lunge-line on Flint. "Here goes."

She led Flint up to the training ring. "Remember, he can be a bit excitable first thing," Amy warned, seeing the Thoroughbred's ears prick and his tail lift as he jogged up the yard.

Claire nodded.

Amy opened the gate and Flint pranced into the ring.

"Be careful, honey," Mrs Whitely said.

Claire walked to the centre of the ring. "Away!" she said to Flint.

With a joyful shy, Flint plunged to the outside of the ring and bucked twice. Amy's heart stopped in her chest. What would Claire do?

"And trot!" Claire said firmly, bringing the whip down on the sand behind him. "Trot on!"

Amy looked at her face. Her eyes were fixed on her horse. Her shoulders square to his, she urged him on. For a moment Flint hesitated and looked as if he was about to plunge again, but Claire brought the whip down on the ground again. "Flint – trot!"

With a toss of his head, the grey gelding obeyed. Amy's hopes lifted. It looked like Claire was going to be OK!

"And canter!" Claire told Flint firmly. He broke into a canter. Claire played out the lunge-line and let him canter in large circles and at last, he started to relax and lower his head.

Amy began to breathe normally again.

"Hey, she's coping really well," Mrs Whitely said.

Claire slowed Flint then turned him before sending him off at a canter on the other rein. Her eyes were focused on the horse and her face shone with a new confidence. After a while, she halted him. "I'll take him off the lunge-line now," she said.

"Are you sure that's wise?" Mrs Whitely said.

Claire nodded. "He'll be fine, Mom."

Unsnapping the lunge-line, she sent Flint to the outside of the ring. "And canter!" she said.

Bound by no rope or line, the beautiful grey horse broke into a canter. His long, Thoroughbred stride seemed to eat up the ground but he steadied himself, his eyes focused on Claire in the middle.

"And trot!" Claire said.

Flint slowed to a trot, obeying his owner's commands – not because he was being dominated or forced to but because he wanted to co-operate with her. Keeping her shoulders in line with his, Claire asked him to turn and sent him at a canter in the other direction. He did so.

Watching Flint so willingly obey the commands and seeing the pride and delight on Claire's face, Amy felt a tearful lump suddenly rise to her throat. There was nothing better than seeing a horse and a human working together as equals – trusting and respecting each other. It was what Heartland was all about.

Hearing a noise behind her, she turned. Ty was standing a little way off. Suddenly he saw Amy looking at him and he walked away.

In the ring, Claire stopped Flint. "What do you think, Mom?" she said, leading him over, her eyes shining.

"It's amazing," Mrs Whitely said in astonishment. "He just did exactly what you told him to."

"I know. He's so wonderful." Claire stopped Flint. "I *can* keep him, can't I, Mom?"

Mrs Whitely smiled. "Yes, you can."

"Oh, thank you!" Claire cried. She threw her arms round Flint's neck. "Did you hear that, Flint? I can keep you!"

Flint whickered and nuzzled her cheek.

Claire looked round in astonishment. "He's never done that before! He must be starting to like me."

As Flint blew on Claire's hair, Amy saw the respect and trust shining in his dark eyes. She smiled. She had a feeling that the worst of Flint and Claire's problems were over.

"Well, now we've decided you're keeping him, I guess we're going to have to start looking for a house with some land," Mrs Whitely said to Claire.

Claire looked at her in surprise. "But we're already renting a house."

Mrs Whitely smiled. "I was talking about a house to *buy*. I really like it around here. It suits my work to stay and I can see it would be good for you – you're obviously happy here." She paused. "And I know it would be nice for you to be nearer your father."

"Oh, Mom, that would be fantastic!" Claire exclaimed. "I'd love to live here permanently." She turned to Amy. "Oh Amy, isn't this great?"

Amy grinned. "You'll have to see Ashley every day!"

"Who cares?" Claire said. She kissed Flint's soft, grey nose. "I've got Flint – nothing else matters."

Amy had just said goodbye to Mrs Whitely and Claire when the phone started to ring. She ran to answer it.

"Hello, Heartland," she said. "Amy Fleming speaking."

"Hi," a woman's voice said. "Is it possible to speak to Ben Stillman, please?"

"You could, but he's out on a ride," Amy said. Suddenly

she caught sight of Ben riding back down the yard. "Actually, he's just got back. Who shall I say is calling?"

"It's his mom."

Amy put the phone down on the side and went to the door. "Ben! It's your mom!"

Ben jumped off Red. "Can you hold him for me?"

"Sure," Amy said.

She took hold of Red's reins and Ben ran down to the kitchen. The horse was still warm from his ride. It looked like Ben had been riding him hard. Deciding to help cool him off, Amy started to walk him round.

Five minutes later, Ben came out of the house.

"What did your mom want?" Amy asked. Suddenly she saw that his face was dark and angry. "Was it bad news?"

"She's not coming!" Ben said.

"Not coming?" Amy echoed.

"To the show."

"Oh, Ben, I'm sorry," Amy said.

Ben grabbed Red's reins. "I was stupid to believe that she really would! She always cancels – always." His face hardened. "Well, from now on I just don't care. She can do what she likes. It's just me and Red – that's all that matters." He put his foot in the stirrup and mounted.

"What are you doing?" Amy said in surprise.

"I'm going to practise for this show," Ben said. "Mom might not be coming, but that's not going to stop me. I don't need her. I don't need anyone."

He clicked his tongue and Red walked forward.

"But Ben, you've only just got back from your ride," Amy protested, walking beside him. "Red's still hot."

Ignoring her, Ben trotted Red away up the yard.

Hearing the clatter of hooves, Ty came out of the feed-room. "What's Ben doing?" he demanded, coming down the yard. "I thought he'd just got back from the trails."

"He has," Amy said. "But he got a phone-call from his mom and he went sort of crazy. He said he's going to jump Red."

"We'll see about that!" Ty said grimly.

He stormed up the yard. Amy hurried after him.

In the training ring, Ben was cantering Red towards a jump. It was high – at least four foot.

"Ben! Stop!" Amy called, running up to the gate.

But Ben ignored her. He brought his whip down on Red's neck and the chestnut cleared the jump easily. Pulling him to a halt, Ben raised the pole another foot.

"What are you doing, Ben?" Ty said, striding into the ring.

"Jumping my horse!" Ben sad through gritted teeth. He swung himself on to Red's back. "Out of my way!"

Ty didn't move. Pulling on Red's reins, Ben cantered the horse past him.

"Ben! No!" Amy said, her heart leaping into her mouth as she saw Ben turn Red into the jump. For one horrible moment she had a vision of her father jumping Pegasus and the pole catching between Pegasus's legs, bringing horse and rider crashing to the ground. Things had gone far enough!

She ran across the sand towards the jump. "Will you *stop*! Red's tired! It's too high for him!"

Ben brought his stick down twice on the chestnut's neck. For one moment Red looked like he was going to take off, but then his courage failed him and he stopped.

"Come on!" Ben shouted, hitting Red's quarters.

The horse panicked and swerved away from the jump, straight into Amy's path. For a moment, all Amy saw was his frightened eyes and foaming mouth, and then she felt Ty grabbing her by her shoulders and pulling her out of the way.

"You idiot!" Ty howled at Ben.

Amy's heart felt like it would burst through her chest, it was hammering so hard. She caught the look of shock on Ben's face and then his eyes darkened again. Turning Red towards the fence, he brought the whip down on Red's quarters.

"Stop that, Ben!" Amy screamed.

Seeing the jump, Red panicked and rose into the air. Taken by surprise, Ben threw himself forward on to Red's neck. It gave Ty the chance he needed. He flung himself across the sand and grabbed Red's reins as the chestnut landed.

Red shot backwards in alarm but Ty hung on. "Steady, boy, Steady!"

"What are you doing?" Ben shouted, recovering his seat and trying to yank the reins off him.

Ty dropped the reins and, grabbing hold of Ben's leg and arm, he pulled him off the saddle.

With a frightened snort, Red shied away. Ben lost his grip and landed on the sand. For a moment, Amy thought Ty was going to hit him.

"Ty, stop!" she cried, racing over.

Ty lowered his arm. He was breathing deeply as he glared at Ben. "Get off this yard," he said, his voice trembling with barely contained fury. "Get off this yard, right now, and don't ever come back!"

Ben got to his feet. His clothes were covered in sand. He stared at Ty for a moment and then, turning swiftly, marched across the sand. Taking Red's reins, he led him out of the ring.

Amy was aghast. She looked at Ty's furious face and then at Ben disappearing down the yard. She stepped forwards.

"Don't go after him, Amy," Ty said intensely.

Amy stopped and looked at him. "I have to. I just *have* to."

Ty's eyes bored into hers. "If you go, I'm leaving," he said. "I've had enough, Amy – I've *compromised* enough. I'm not prepared to stand by when I see cruelty like that – not even for you."

"What do you mean?" Amy whispered.

Just then there was the sound of shouting. Ben came running up to the gate. "Amy!" he yelled. "Amy! It's Red! Come quick!"

Chapter Ten

Amy didn't think twice. She ran to the gate.

"Red's gone down in his stall!" Ben gasped.

Amy raced down the yard. When she got to Red's stall, she saw that the chestnut was trying to roll. "Colic!" she said, grabbing the halter from his door. "Quick! Get him up!"

Ben had taken Red's saddle and bridle off. Grabbing Red by his mane, he urged him to his feet. The chestnut scrambled up, but almost at once his legs began to buckle again. "Walk him round," she said, doing the halter up quickly. "He mustn't roll violently like that or he might twist a gut. I'll get Ty."

"Ty won't help!" Ben said. "Just call the vet."

"I'll get Ty first," Amy said. She saw Ben's face. "If a horse is in trouble, Ty will help – no matter who its owner is."

She raced back up the yard. Ty was walking down from the training ring, his face set.

"Ty!" Amy gasped. "Red's got colic. It looks bad. Ben's walking him round." She grabbed his hand. "Please, Ty! You can't turn your back on him."

Ty stared at her. "You honestly think that I'd refuse to help a horse in trouble?"

"No ... I ... no," Amy began to stammer.

"Well, thanks a lot, Amy," Ty said angrily. He pulled away from her and strode down the yard, but not before Amy had seen the feeling of utter betrayal in his eyes.

Ben was walking Red around the yard. The horse's sides were damp with sweat. When Ben saw Ty, his face tightened. But Ty ignored his expression. "Have you any idea what could have caused it?" he demanded.

For a moment, Ben looked like he wasn't going to answer but then his concern for his horse overcame him. "None. He was fine out on the trails," he said, stopping Red.

"Did he eat anything while he was out?" Ty asked.

"No – well, nothing that could harm him. I stopped for a bit and let him graze on some grass at the side of a field."

"Not cut grass?" Ty said quickly.

"Of course not!" Ben said angrily. "And I didn't let him drink a troughful of water after it either. I'm not stupid. I do know what causes colic, you know!"

"Calm down, Ben!" Amy said. "Ty's just trying to help."

Ben ran a hand through his hair. "Yeah, OK. I'm sorry." Red's legs started to fold again. "Up, boy!" Ben cried, making him move again.

"Amy, will you call Scott?" Ty said.

"Sure."

Amy ran inside. But the receptionist at Scott's veterinary centre told her that Scott was out on call. "I'll get the message to him as quickly as possible," she told Amy.

"Please do," Amy begged, looking out of the window and seeing Red kick at the ground and look at his flanks.

As she put the phone down, Lou came into the kitchen. "What's happened?" she said, seeing Amy's worried face.

Amy quickly explained.

"That sounds bad," Lou said. "Is there anything I can do?"

Amy shook her head. "Not really – although you could ring the centre back in ten minutes and see if they've got through to Scott and if they know how long he's going to be."

"Sure," Lou said. "And I'll get Grandpa."

Amy hurried outside and told Ben and Ty what was happening. "They're trying to get in touch with Scott, but he's out on call."

Grandpa and Lou came hurrying out of the house. Jack Bartlett's eyes swept over the distressed horse. "It's colic, right?" he said to Ty.

Ty nodded. "But we don't know what's caused it."

Suddenly Red seemed to stagger. "He's getting worse!" Ben said.

"Keep him walking," Jack Bartlett instructed.

Ben moved Red on. "I can't believe this has happened so quickly," he said. "Colic doesn't normally get bad so fast, does it?"

"Maybe it's not just colic," Ty said thoughtfully.

Ben turned on him. "Of course it's colic! You can see the way he keeps trying to roll."

"What else do you think it could it be, Ty?" Jack Bartlett said quickly.

"It could be poisoning," Ty said. "Colic might be just one of the symptoms."

"Poisoning!" Amy echoed, her heart dropping.

Ty was already hurrying to Red's head. "Hold him still," he said to Ben. He opened the horse's mouth. "I'm right – I'm sure I am. Look at his gums – they're inflamed!" He turned to Ben. "What's he been eating?"

"Nothing – only grass!" Ben said desperately. "And I checked it out. There was nothing in it. It was just plain grass at the side of a field."

Amy's heart pounded. She knew that when treating cases of poisoning you had to act quickly, but it was also vital to discover exactly what type of poisoning it was so that the right remedy could be used. But how could they find out what Red had eaten before it was too late?

"Which field were you in?" Ty demanded.

"I don't know," Ben said. "It was out to the south. It looked like it had just been seeded."

"Just seeded?" Ty repeated.

"Do you think you know what the poison might be, Ty?" Grandpa said.

Ty didn't answer. Instead he raised a hand quickly in front of Red's face. The chestnut shied back clumsily. Ty nodded. "That's it," he said grimly.

"What?" Amy demanded.

"Mercury poisoning," Ty said.

Ben stared at Ty. "But Red hasn't been anywhere near any mercury!"

"Organic mercury compounds are sometimes used as seed dressings," Ty said. "It's my bet that the field had been treated and the seed dressing had got on to the grass at the side."

Ben's face paled. "But mercury's really toxic."

Grandpa spoke quickly. "Is there anything we can do, Ty? Can we drench him? Give him something?"

"If it *is* mercury poisoning then we have to get the mercury out of his system as fast as we can," Ty replied. "If we don't it may well cause kidney failure. We can try drenching him with a saturated sodium bicarbonate solution. That should help clear the mercury out."

"But what if it isn't mercury poisoning?" Amy whispered, looking at Red and then back at Ty. "What if the sodium bicarbonate doesn't help – or even makes things worse?"

"It's a risk," Ty admitted. "But if we wait for Scott to get here, it might be too late." He looked at Ben. "It's your choice, Ben."

Ben hesitated. Red groaned and his knees buckled. "Treat him!" he suddenly said, as Red collapsed on the ground. "I'll take the risk!"

"Amy, Jack – can you help Ben get Red into his stall?" Ty said, starting to run up the yard. "I'll make up the solution. Lou, can you ring the vet's again and say that this is a real emergency?"

Everyone did as Ty asked. Amy, Grandpa and Ben forced Red to his feet. His legs were unsteady but they just about managed to get him into his stall. Ben's face was pale as he turned Red in circles to stop him lying down. "I'll never forgive myself if anything happens to him," he said. "Never!"

Ty appeared with three old plastic bottles filled with a saturated solution of sodium bicarbonate.

"It's OK. You can let him lie down," he said. "Just don't let him roll."

Ben let Red sink down on to the straw. Ty knelt down beside the horse's head and opened the first bottle. "Come on, boy," he said, tilting the horse's head back. "I know you're not going to like this but I'm afraid we've got no choice."

Red struggled to get his head away, as Ty began to tip the liquid down his throat.

"Here, I'll hold him," Ben said, moving swiftly to Ty's side and steadying Red's head. With Ben there, caressing his neck and face, Red calmed down.

"Don't hold his head too high or he might choke," Ty said.

"Come on, boy," Amy whispered, kneeling beside him and

stroking his hot neck. "You're going to get better!" She glanced at Lou and Grandpa who were standing by the stall door watching tensely.

Ty finished one bottle and started on the other. "Are you sure this is right?" Ben said, looking at the stream of liquid being poured steadily down Red's throat.

"We have to try and wash the poison out," Ty said. He finished the second bottle. "OK, let him rest for a few minutes."

Ben let go of Red's head and, making a wisp from some straw, began to dry Red's sweating sides.

Amy saw the horse look uneasily round at his stomach.

"It's OK, boy," she said, moving up to his head and starting to work T-Touch circles on his ears and face. "It's going to be just fine."

Amy's fingers worked skilfully. Horses who were ill often responded well to ear-work. Gradually, Red stopped looking at his stomach.

"He seems to like that," Ben said, coming and joining her. "Will you show me what to do?"

Amy explained how to do the circles and Ben took her place at the Red's head.

Amy felt the chestnut's sides. His skin was still hot and damp, his flanks trembling slightly.

"His breathing's quite shallow," she said in a low voice to Ty.

"Let's drench him again," Ty said, looking worried.

"I'll fetch you some more," Grandpa said.

And so, alternately drenching and using T-Touch circles, Amy, Ty and Ben worked on Red, talking to him, encouraging him and soothing him.

"Come on, boy," Ben pleaded. "You can make it!" He turned to Ty. "Isn't there anything else you can give him?

Ty shook his head.

Ben buried his head in his hands. "He's got to get better."

"Just keep working," Ty said grimly

Just then, there was the sound of the phone ringing. "I'll get it!" Lou said, hurrying away.

A few minutes later, she came running back. "That was the vet's – Scott's on his way. They think he should be about twenty minutes." She looked at Ty in concern. "Will that be soon enough?"

"I hope so," Ty said.

Ben squared his shoulders. "It will be!" He stared to work on Red's ears again. "It has to be."

Grandpa reappeared in the stall doorway and looked at the sodden, soiled bed. "He could do with some clean straw. Come on, Lou – give me a hand."

As Lou and Grandpa fetched some clean straw and began to spread a thick layer over the bed, Amy felt Red's sides. Suddenly, she realized that the skin under her fingers seemed less hot and no new patches of sweat appeared to be breaking out. "Hey!" she said. "I think he's calming down. In fact, I'm sure."

The others looked at Red. His head was resting on the straw still but his eyes had lost the panic-stricken look of earlier and his nostrils were no longer flaring with every breath.

"You're right!" Ben said. "Come on, boy!" he said in delight. "You're going to make it."

Amy set to work with renewed vigour. *Oh, please*, she prayed, *please let this mean that Red is going to pull through*.

Twenty minutes later, there was the sound of car tyres screeching to a halt outside the house.

"Scott!" Amy cried in relief as the vet appeared in the stall doorway.

"I came as fast as I could," Scott said, kneeling down next to Red.

"I think it's mercury poisoning," Ty said quickly. He explained about the grass that Red had eaten. "He was showing signs of nervousness and lack of co-ordination and had severe colic. We didn't know when you'd be here so I took a chance and treated him – I've been drenching him with sodium bicarbonate solution."

Scott stroked Red's neck. "You did the right thing. In fact, your prompt action might well have saved his life." He looked at Ben. "He's your horse, right?"

Ben nodded. "Is he going to be OK?" he asked anxiously

"I'll inject him with some calcium disodium versenate," Scott said, checking Red's mouth as he spoke. "It'll chelate any remaining mercury so that it can be excreted harmlessly. And I'll take a sample of his stomach contents for analysis. But it looks like mercury poisoning to me." He stood up. "I'll get my things from the car."

"So he'll make a full recovery?" Jack Bartlett asked.

Scott nodded. "He'll need several more injections over the next couple of days, but I think we'll soon have him on his feet again."

As Scott hurried out of the stall, Amy sat back in the straw, feeling half dazed with relief. Suddenly all the tension that had been building up inside her over the course of the afternoon overwhelmed her. She gave a sob.

Ty and Ben looked round in surprise.

"Hey," Ty said, moving swiftly beside her and putting his arm around her shoulders. "You heard Scott. Red's going to be OK."

Amy nodded and sniffed. She felt so mixed-up and confused. She was delighted that Scott thought Red was going to be fine, but that didn't wipe away the events of the afternoon.

When Scott had finished treating Red, he started to put his things back in his bag. "Looks like he's been in the wars," he said, pointing to the whip marks still visible from earlier. "How did he get those?"

Amy glanced at Ben. His face was bright red. "Um ... I..."

"Oh, they happened when he was turned out in the field,"

Ty said quickly. "You know, just regular scuffling with the other horses."

Amy saw Ben look at Ty in astonishment.

"Oh, right," Scott said, straightening up.

Grandpa had gone back to the house, but Lou still stood by the stall door. "Would you like to come in for a drink?" she asked Scott.

Scott smiled at her. "Thanks," he said picking up his bag. "That would be good."

Lou opened the door for him and they walked down the yard together.

Ben turned to Ty. "Thanks," he said quietly.

Ty shrugged.

"I mean it, Ty," Ben went on. "And not just for telling Scott that Red got those marks in the field and not from me. Thanks for everything – for realizing what was wrong with Red and for doing what you did. If it hadn't been for you, Red might have died." He crouched down in the straw and stroked the chestnut horse. "Red means more to me than all the world," he said quietly. "He's the only thing I have."

Ty frowned. Amy saw it and so did Ben.

He laughed bitterly. "Oh, I know you think I'm real lucky – that I've got it all, but it isn't as simple as that. My dad ran off when I was ten, and after that I found it really hard to settle down at school. I started mucking about and getting into trouble. My mom couldn't cope with the way I was behaving and she sent me to live with my aunt." He looked Ty straight in the eye. "It felt like she was getting rid of me." Ben shook his head. "My aunt's been great, but she's always made it clear that she's got her own life to lead – her own agenda. I owe a lot to her in that she got me interested in horses, and she gave me Red, but when she told me that she wanted me to come and work here I resented it. I guess I felt rejected again." He turned back to Red. "Look, I know I haven't handled things well at all, and that I'm not the only one with problems ... it's just I haven't felt like I've belonged anywhere for a long time." He looked up at Amy and Ty. "So you see, my life hasn't been as simple as you probably thought."

"Actually, I ... I knew about your parents getting divorced," Amy admitted. "Lisa told Lou." She felt Ty look at her.

"Did you all know?" Ben said, obviously embarrassed.

Amy shook her head. "Ty didn't."

Ben looked at Ty. "Well, now you do," he said. "And now, maybe you can understand why I've acted like a jerk. I've got some issues that I need to deal with, and sometimes I feel like the only one that cares about me at all is Red."

"Ben!" Amy exclaimed. "That's just not true. Life isn't as black and white as that. There were reasons why your mom sent you to live with your aunt – some good, some bad. Just like when Lisa sent you here. She probably did it mostly because she thought you'd get something out of it. She definitely cares about you."

"Maybe," Ben said. He smiled. "She got me Red, anyway."

He gently touched the horse's face. "Training him was the first thing I was ever good at. My aunt bought him for me when he was three. No one else could ride him, but I did. And that's why competing him is so important. When I'm in the ring with him and we win and people clap and cheer, it's like suddenly I matter – I'm a success."

All at once, Amy began to understand why Ben seemed so driven by the urge to win. He didn't just like it – he *needed* it.

Ben sighed. "You know, although there's been ups and downs since I got here, I have enjoyed it – I'll be sorry to go."

"Go?" Amy said in surprise.

"Yeah, go." He looked at her. "I know you're not going to let me stay after how I've been acting. And what I did to Red was wrong." He shook his head. "It was more than wrong – I was upset and I took it out on him. There's no excuse for that."

"No, there isn't," Amy said honestly. "But if you're really sorry, then we can try and work it out. "But it's not up to me. It's Ty's decision." She looked at Ty who was staring intently at Ben.

Ben averted his gaze. "But I thought you'd hate me for what I did," he said to Amy.

"I hate *what* you did," Amy said. "But not you." She looked at Red. "I know you love him."

Ben nodded. "I do, and I'm going to try and regain his

trust." He stroked Red's mane. "Seeing him so ill, I suddenly realized how much he meant to me and I also realized how right you were. I don't want Red to obey me because he's scared, I want him to obey me because he wants to." He met Ty's steady gaze. "If I can't stay, I'll understand. But whatever happens, I want you to know, I've learnt an invaluable lesson here."

Amy looked at Ty, willing him to say what she wanted to hear.

He nodded. "It's OK," he said quietly. "You can stay, Ben."

Amy felt a rush of relief as she saw Ben's eyes light up.

"I'll work hard," he said quickly. "I'll learn fast. I want to be a real part of the Heartland team."

Suddenly, Red nickered softly, half lifting his head from the straw.

They all looked at each other

"Hey, boy," Ben said softly, reaching out to stroke him. "You feeling better?"

Amy swallowed as she saw Red lift his nose to Ben's face and begin to nuzzle his forehead. The horse's eyes were full of love. Despite everything, Red had forgiven his beloved master.

Leaving Ben and Red in the stall, Amy and Ty went outside. "So, how long have you known about Ben's past?" Ty said when they were out of earshot of the stall.

"For about two weeks," Amy admitted. "I couldn't tell

you. Lou made me promise not to. She said it would be hard for Ben if he found out that we all knew. But it's been *so* hard keeping it from you. It's been driving me crazy."

"Lou was probably right," Ty said. He ran a hand through his hair. "Though I have to admit, it was really difficult knowing that there was something you weren't telling me." He shook his head. "Still, now I know, I guess I understand *why* you were sticking up for Ben."

Looking at his untidy hair and the tiredness in his eyes that reflected the stress of the afternoon, Amy was unable to contain herself any longer. "Oh, Ty," she said desperately. "Please don't leave. I need you here – we all do. Heartland wouldn't be Heartland without you!"

"Leave?" Ty said. "What are you talking about?"

"I know you're thinking about going to Green Briar," Amy rushed on. "I heard you on the phone to Val Grant. I heard you say you'd think about it and let her know. But please, please don't go!"

There was a silence. "Amy," Ty said, his eyes searching hers. "Tell me honestly – did you ever think, even for one second, that I wouldn't help Red because of what had happened between Ben and I?"

Amy didn't hesitate. "No," she said.

"Then you should also know that I would never, ever consider leaving Heartland to go and work at Green Briar," Ty said. "I only said I'd leave earlier because I was so mad at you."

"But I heard..."

"You heard me say that I would let Val Grant know," Ty said. "If you'd heard the whole of that conversation, you'd have realized that I was saying I would let her know if I changed my mind and decided to switch jobs. I'd already made it clear at the start of the conversation that I wasn't leaving Heartland."

"So you're not going?" Amy echoed, as the words started to sink in.

"No," Ty said, shaking his head. "I'm not."

"Oh, Ty!" Amy said, her eyes starting to shine with relief and delight. "I'm so glad! I hated the thought of trying to carry on without you."

"Well, you don't have to." Ty took her hand and looked into her eyes. "My future's here at Heartland, Amy – with you."